TRADING
TIME

OWEN MARTIN
TRADING TIME

Red Door

Published by RedDoor
www.reddoorpress.co.uk

© 2020 Owen Martin

The right of Owen Martin to be identified as author
of this Work has been asserted by him in accordance with
sections 77 and 78 of the Copyright, Designs and Patents Act
1988

ISBN 978-1-913062-32-3

A CIP catalogue record for this book is available from
the British Library

Cover design: Dissect Designs

Typesetting: Tutis Innovative E-Solutions Pte Ltd

Printed and bound in Denmark by Nørhaven

To JDG

Chapter One

By the time Gabriel opened his eyes, his mother, Ana, had already dispatched the two youngest children to school and the three older ones had disappeared from their mattresses to search for paying work – or at least that was what they had told their mother. The freshness of the early morning had dissipated and the air was stiflingly hard to breathe. Ana had also been down the mountainside to fetch water and buy bread, as she did every morning. Gabriel could see her silhouetted against the few slithers of light making it into the gloom of the room. Her legs were powerful from climbing the hundreds of steps of the favela virtually every day of her adult life, her shoulders were broad from carrying everything the family needed up from the city. She was only forty years old but she looked more like a woman of sixty.

She was leaning over the stove making coffee in the battered, stained metal pot she had used all Gabriel's life. The air conditioner that João, Gabriel's father, had proudly wedged into the one downstairs window, blocking out virtually all the sunlight, had stopped functioning twelve years ago, several months after João's body was found at the bottom of the hill, and the heat was making Ana perspire. Every few seconds she had to wipe the sweat from her eyes in order to see what she was doing.

"Sorry, Mama," Gabriel said, stretching like a cat as he rose in one fluid movement from the hot narrow mattress which served as a bed for him and two of his brothers. "You should have woken me."

"You need your sleep," she said, smiling fondly at her eldest son, proudly watching his gleaming brown torso as he walked towards her through the gloom. "Me, I'm awake anyway because of my aches and pains."

She never resented it when he slept in on his rare days off because she knew how hard he worked to keep the family fed, tending the gardens of the rich during the day, waiting on tables in restaurants along the Copacabana at night. She had heard him coming in at three that morning, picking his way over the sleeping bodies of his siblings to find his own space on the mattresses.

He put his arms around her and kissed her wet forehead. "Today is the day I will get the money," he said. "When it arrives I will buy you the softest bed in Rio."

"You need to take care of your grandmother first," she said, gesturing towards the skinny old woman hunched in the corner of the room. With her opaque eyes staring blindly into the darkness, she was grumbling quietly to herself because she believed she had lived too long and was angry to find she had woken up to spend yet another day being a burden to her widowed daughter-in-law. There were many old women in the

2

area who had outlived their children, but that did not make it feel any less unnatural.

"Don't worry" – Gabriel squeezed Ana tightly, playfully pinning her arms to her sides – "there will be enough money to buy beds for everyone."

"Oh, yes?" she asked, half-heartedly trying to wriggle free from his embrace. "And where do you suggest we put all these wonderful soft beds?"

Gabriel looked around the room at the recently vacated mattresses and laughed. "I'm going to build us another floor, just like Papa always said he would, and there will be plenty of room for all of us, and Isabella too – and all the grandchildren we are going to give you."

The look of amusement left his mother's face. "Stop talking nonsense," she snapped. "There is only one way to make that sort of money. Do you want to end up dead in a ditch like your poor father?"

"There are other ways to make money, honest ways," Gabriel assured her as he released her. "Don't worry, Mama, I have plans. You can relax, everything is going to get better soon."

"Pah," his mother responded, turning back to the stove and taking her anger out by banging the coffee pot around. "You sound exactly like your father. He was always making promises. Always believing the lies that people told him. Always dreaming that tomorrow his luck would change!"

She immediately regretted snapping at him because they both knew he was nothing like his father. João would never have been willing to work every day and night for the pittances that Gabriel's various employers paid. João had always claimed it was because of his pride that such menial labours were below him, that life was too short to be spent slaving for people more stupid than himself, but Ana knew it was because he was idle and believed that he deserved to earn his money without making any physical effort or suffering any physical pain. That was why he had ended up mixing with the wrong people – the sort of people who promised easy money but always exacted a terrible price for those promises.

It worried her when Gabriel talked about bringing home unexplained amounts of money, because experience told her that for people like them there were only a few ways for that to happen: stealing, selling drugs or selling sex. She didn't want her wonderful boy mixed up in any of those businesses and she knew that the worst people in the neighbourhood were anxious to recruit him because of his popularity and his work ethic. His obvious beauty and easy charm made her nervous as well as making her proud. She could not imagine how the family would survive if anything bad were to happen to Gabriel.

"Enough, Mama!" His voice was sharper than he meant it to be. He didn't like it when anyone criticised João, even her. It exploded something deep inside him. Feelings of loyalty that he would now never be able to express to the man himself were mixed with anger at the injustice of a world where his father could be murdered and the police wouldn't even bother to come to the scene.

When Gabriel was sixteen, Paulo, one of the more dangerous neighbourhood boys, had dared to suggest that João was a police stooge and that was why he had been killed. Gabriel had pulled a knife and slashed the other boy's face, narrowly missing his left eye, reacting before he even realised he was that angry. Paulo would carry the scar for the rest of his life, which meant that Gabriel knew he would have to shoulder the guilt for the rest of his life too, but at least it meant he received respect from the others. That one moment of uncontrolled fury, that one flash of steel and the stream of blood that followed, witnessed by at least a dozen other people, had anointed him with a reputation for being someone to fear and treat respectfully, someone who could not be pushed over his limits without unleashing consequences. The fact that the scar was so visible on Paulo's otherwise unblemished cheek meant that Gabriel hadn't been challenged again and hadn't needed to remind anyone of the fury boiling below the surface inside him, or to prove again the speed with which he could strike – at least not yet.

His mother understood all that – she had been a street child herself after all – but she also knew that it was only a matter of time before one of the local killers realised Gabriel was actually a gentle soul and then they would challenge or insult him again and Lord alone knew what the outcome would be. Young men were always testing their strength against the strength of those around them. It was in their nature. She had seen the way Paulo glowered at Gabriel, his eyes dark with hatred above the vivid red scar, and she heard from the other women that he was now working for the worst of the worst, growing stronger and more ruthless with every year that he managed to survive. One day he was bound to decide the time was right to exact his revenge – an eye for an eye maybe, or perhaps worse.

Every day when she heard screaming outside the house or the pounding of running feet, she expected to be brought the news that she had lost her eldest son, or that he had been brutally mutilated in some way. She wasn't sure that she could bear the pain of another night like the one when the women came to the door to share the news that her beloved João was dead, his throat sliced open from ear to ear. A couple of months later she discovered he had left her pregnant with their final child.

"Here, give this to your grandmother."

She handed him a chipped bowl-shaped cup that had once belonged to a café in town, filled with milky coffee, and some pieces of bread which she had chopped small enough for the old woman to be able to chew with her gums.

Gabriel squatted down next to his grandmother and touched her hand so that she would know he was there. He gently placed the coffee cup in her right hand and the pieces of bread in her left.

"You are more an angel than a man," the old woman croaked.

She said the same thing every day, several times a day, and Gabriel always gave the same reply. "An angel descended from a goddess," he said, and she rewarded him with a toothless grin.

"Gabriel!" For a second he didn't recognise the sound of his own name being called from the alley outside. The voice was so sweet and musical it was more like the birdsong that sometimes penetrated through the more discordant sounds of the favela, emanating from the songbirds in cramped cages that so many men liked to carry around with them and hang in their windows whenever they were at home.

Ana heard the call too and made a clicking sound with her tongue, which would have registered her disapproval to anyone who might be listening. Gabriel heard the click of his mother's tongue but it didn't upset him. He knew that her dislike of his relationship with Isabella was not personal. Who could possibly disapprove of a girl so sweet natured and so beautiful? Ana disapproved of Isabella because she knew that Gabriel was in love with her and she knew that young men who were in love with beautiful women often made big mistakes. They wanted to impress the objects of their adoration and they wanted to look after them and protect them, all of which required the acquisition of money. In the favelas the acquisition of money always required the taking of risks. Ana was happy to think that her son was blessed enough to have been given the opportunity to kiss such a beautiful young face, but frightened as to where his desires might lead him once the kissing was no longer enough to satisfy his manly urges. Other men would be wanting to take her away from him and some would be willing to resort to violence to achieve that goal. She could hardly blame Gabriel for putting himself in such danger because Isabella was a truly sublime creature – her slim, golden body brimming with good health and good nature, her flawless face radiant from the joy of being in love – but still Ana was fearful of what the future might hold for such a noticeably beautiful and blessed young couple.

"Gabriel!" The siren voice called again. Gabriel knew she wouldn't come in. She was too respectful towards Ana to enter the house uninvited and Ana would never want that. No one said anything, but they all knew instinctively that Ana was ashamed of the level of poverty in which she had been forced to bring up her children. She should have been proud to have brought up such strong, healthy, honest children in such difficult circumstances – and in many ways she was proud – but she was also aware of just how dark and foul smelling the house was because there was no proper drainage and no matter how many hours a day she spent scrubbing the floors she could never expel those smells. Isabella came from a poor family too, but they all had jobs in the city and their combined wages had meant they could extend their house over the years, putting windows in the walls, albeit protected by stout bars, and water tanks on the roof so that they could wash themselves and their home to expunge the odours of poverty. Isabella could afford to buy trainers for her feet and her skin and hair smelled as good as they looked, her perfume attracting boys wherever she went, like bees to sweet pollen.

"I have to go, Mama," Gabriel said, kissing his grandmother and mother as he passed, a brilliant white smile flashing across his handsome face. "Tonight I will have a big surprise for you. You will like it, I promise."

"Pah." Ana dismissed him with a cursory wave as he slipped past.

Isabella was sitting on the steps outside, already surrounded by several young men, including Paulo, who had heard her calling out to Gabriel and came just to be near her and stare at her for a few moments, imagining what it would feel like to be allowed to touch such a woman. They all pulled back a few inches when they saw Gabriel emerging through the door, which was so low he virtually had to crouch on all fours to get through, like an animal appearing from a burrow beneath a tree. He straightened up into the narrow band of sunlight that had made it onto the steps past the crowded buildings above, filtered through the hundreds of knotted electricity and telephone wires that linked the crumbling walls together, sparking and crackling off one another whenever someone touched them. Gabriel felt the familiar frisson of excitement seeing Isabella's face light up at his approach. Every muscle in his body ached to hold her close and the scent of her skin when he kissed her soft lips made him feel dizzy with desire.

"Hey, Gabriel," one of the younger boys said, stepping back respectfully to allow the couple some room, "you want to meet with the man today?"

"Nah." Gabriel didn't take his eyes off Isabella's as he spoke. "Not today. We've got important things to do."

"You say that every day," Paulo growled. "He's starting to think you don't want to talk to him. He's taking it personally."

"I'll talk to him," Gabriel said, knowing that there would eventually come a time when he would have to tell them all that he wanted nothing to do with their money-making schemes, all of which involved flouting the law and risking death or arrest, "but not today. Today I've got big plans with my girl."

Isabella's smile grew even broader and he couldn't resist kissing her again, even with half a dozen pairs of envious eyes boring into the back of his head.

"He's going to be pissed off with you," Paulo warned, but Gabriel pretended not to hear.

When he was this close to Isabella nothing else in the world seemed to matter and he felt full of confidence about the future. The touch of her fingers on his face as she gazed into his eyes, her lips still parted after their kiss, made him feel like he could take on the whole world and win. They were going to be together all day and by the time they got back home that evening they would have ten thousand dollars. It might be small change to Paulo's boss, the man who ran that part of the favela with such ruthless greed, but it was probably more than Gabriel's father earned in his entire adult life. It meant that they would be able to put another floor on the family home and install a water tank on the roof. Once that was done, he and Isabella could get married and live together. He could already imagine the children they would have, visualising them running up and down the stairs, being scolded and spoiled by his mother who would live below them with a comfortable bed and a chair and an air conditioner that actually worked. All of this was going to be within reach by the time they got home that night.

With a casual wave to the boys they were leaving behind, he put his arm around Isabella's slender bare shoulders; their hips pressed close as they danced down the steps in unison towards the only street in the area that was wide enough to take traffic. Every step they took was watched from the shadows by people who would report back to other people, who they were afraid of and wanted to please. Nothing went unnoticed in the favela because every piece of information might hold a key someone could use to escape.

The bus that carried them on down the mountainside towards their bright new future belched black smoke from its exhaust every time the driver touched the accelerator.

Sitting close to one another on the bus, their fingers tightly entwined, thighs pressed together on the narrow seat, they were so wrapped up in one another and their big dreams that they were unaware of the heat and smell of the other bodies crowded in around them. They were oblivious to all the conversations going on above their heads as they talked about what they were going to do with the money, both of them nervous about what might lie in store for them at the end of the bus ride but neither wanting to admit it. When you have nothing to lose, you have no choice but to take risks.

The advertisement that the sniggering man in the restaurant had drawn to Gabriel's attention had seemed too good to be true. When he and Isabella had gone to the brief interview with the woman in the white coat, who they assumed was a doctor because of her confident, businesslike manner and the stethoscope that hung casually around her neck, the process had appeared reassuringly professional and hygienic, even though they had been sitting in an anonymous room behind a travel agency that appeared to have virtually no customers coming through its doors. The promises they were given had seemed far too good to be true, but what had seemed like an impossible fantasy at first was now realistically within their reach. Why shouldn't they be due the sort of lucky break that had previously only seemed to happen to other people? Maybe now it was finally their turn.

The money they had been promised as a fee for the procedure still sounded out of proportion for what they were being asked to do, but both of them had limited experience of the world the rich inhabited. Maybe this was just small change to the people who had paid for the advertisement. When Gabriel waited on tables he was often shocked by how casually the customers paid hundreds or even thousands of dollars or reals for a meal, or left a tip which was enough for him to buy groceries for the whole family for several days. Isabella worked as a chambermaid in one of the beachside hotels and was amazed by the things that guests would discard in the rooms, and by the dollars they would sometimes slide into her hand for the smallest of services, like the provision of an extra towel or pillow. So why would such people not be willing to pay them ten thousand dollars for a few hours spent lying on a bed in a shiny clean clinic? They felt like they were moving into a new world where money was never a problem, and the possibilities of such a world thrilled them and made them feel optimistic for the future.

Inside the crowded bus they were both aware of their own youth and attractiveness. Most of the other passengers were old or so worn down by poverty and hard work that they might as well have been old. They both expected to be stared at and admired when amongst such people and were never disappointed. Isabella was used to avoiding the lascivious stares and groping hands of men of all ages. Often it was the old men, the ones who looked like her grandfather, who were the worst as they tried to recapture some moment of ecstasy they had experienced or imagined in their youth; not wanting to believe that they would never experience such wonderful things again.

Once they got off the bus, however, and were walking the two blocks to the tower which housed the clinic they had been told to report to, Gabriel became increasingly conscious of the shabbiness of his clothes, the thinness of the flip-flops that clung to his dusty feet, and that his hair had been cut by his mother with her one kitchen knife. Men still ran their greedy eyes over Isabella as she passed, but everyone looked right through him, seeing just another poor boy from the slums, maybe even fearing him a little, assuming that he might be hungry, perhaps carrying a blade, and desperate enough to want to take by force whatever they had in their pockets and handbags. Everyone around them looked so chic and well groomed, their clothes sharply pressed and their feet encased in dazzling white trainers or shiny leather shoes as they went purposefully about their business, filling their days with appointments, meals, shopping and other pleasures.

He knew exactly the sort of designer clothes he would buy once he had money in his pocket because he had seen them in the windows of the sort of stores he did not yet feel confident enough to enter. They wouldn't be like the uniforms the restaurants gave him to wear for work, with the shoes that never quite fitted and pinched his feet, giving him new blisters at the end of every long shift, and which would be handed out to someone else on the shifts he wasn't working. He knew the designers' names from the billboards he glimpsed from the buses and the magazines that eventually made their way down to the favelas once they had been thrown out by the people who actually bought the goods being advertised. From Gucci to Ralph Lauren he had planned his future wardrobe as carefully as Isabella had planned the dress she would wear on their wedding day.

Gabriel tightened his grip on Isabella's slim fingers, as if to reassure her but actually more to reassure himself. He would not have had the courage to come to this place on his own, but when he was with her he felt he could do anything and was anxious to show her how brave he was. Today, he told himself, everything was going to change for them. They were going to

13

make the seed money that would lift them out of poverty and give them a chance to lead decent, clean lives. Eventually they would be able to get themselves and their families out of the favela altogether and then they would all be living in streets like this, fitting in with people whose lives were successful and comfortable and safe. He felt Isabella's tiny fingers squeezing back and knew that the same thoughts were going through her head. His heart fluttered, partly with the intensity of his love for her and partly with excitement at the thought of whatever was about to happen.

They felt like trespassers from another world as they found the building with the right number emblazoned on one of its pillars and made their way through the newly polished glass doors into the marble foyer. A uniformed doorman stood behind a desk, in front of a board bearing the names of all the businesses housed in the tower. The board told them that the clinic was on the twenty-second floor. He greeted them with polite words, but his voice was cold and his eyes were suspicious as he enquired who they wanted to see and what their names were. They told him they had an appointment and he consulted a list on a computer screen that was sunk into the polished black surface of his desk. If he was surprised to find their names there, he hid it with professional skill.

"Take the elevator to twenty-two," he told them. "Someone will meet you there."

He watched impassively as they made the long walk to the bank of elevators, as if he thought they might make a run for it in another direction if he took his eyes off them, enjoying the way Isabella's body moved inside the light dress and the smooth curve of her bare brown calves. He then picked up the phone and informed someone that they were on their way.

The walls of the elevator were mirrored from floor to ceiling, and as it hummed silently upwards Gabriel felt his heartbeat quicken again. He studied the reflections and saw how beautiful his woman was and imagined how it would be when they were married. The pictures in his head brought tears to his eyes. He could barely believe that he would soon be able to live with her in his own house, holding her close every night, kissing her whenever he wanted. He hardly dared to breathe in case he broke the spell, and then the mirrored doors slid open to reveal a small oriental woman in a white coat waiting for them. It was a different woman to the one who had interviewed them in the room behind the travel agency.

She would have been pretty had it not been for her severe expression and the narrow rimless glasses she had perched on the end of her nose. Her hair was pinned up in a tight bun at the back of her head. It was almost as if she was deliberately trying to hide her youth and beauty beneath an aura of gravitas. Gabriel gave her a smile that usually melted the heart of any woman who beheld it, but she merely looked down at her clipboard and asked their names again. Satisfied that they were on her list, she turned on her elegant heels and instructed them to follow her through a door that clicked open when she pressed a plastic card against an illuminated pad. The card was attached to a lanyard which hung around her slim neck on a length of white silk.

Everything on the other side of the door was white, from the carpets and couches to the blinds that kept out all natural light and all signs of city street life below. The only things that weren't white were a small black coffee machine and a tray of multicoloured pods.

"Help yourselves to coffee," she said without breaking her stride, "and take a seat. We will be with you in a moment."

Another door closed behind her and they were left standing in the middle of the white room feeling shabby and embarrassingly colourful, not daring to touch the coffee machine for fear of causing a spillage and blemishing the purity of their surroundings. They exchanged nervous looks and perched together on the edge of one of the couches, still holding hands like small children being taken out of school for a walk by their teacher. The cushions were unexpectedly soft and Isabella made a note to herself that when she had the money she would buy some cushions just like these for their new home together. It probably wouldn't be wise to have white ones because everyone who came and went from the house would be leaving dirty marks on them, but one day she would live in a room as clean and quiet, as soft and comfortable as this one.

"Is this going to hurt?" Isabella whispered.

"I don't think so," he replied, wanting to reassure her but having no idea if he was telling the truth. "Maybe the prick of a needle, but I think they give us something to make us sleepy first."

"Will they be giving us cash today?"

"That's what they promised."

"Do you trust them?"

He was about to say that he did and then realised that he really didn't have any idea if he did or not. He shrugged his shoulders. "They won't want us making a noise in here. I think they will pay us what they have promised."

Silence fell again and Gabriel could feel Isabella's pulse beating fast beneath the soft skin of her fragile wrist. A few minutes later the same woman returned and invited them to follow her once more, this time into a clinical room, where two surgical tables had been prepared for them and a variety of waiting instruments gleamed in shiny silver kidney dishes. She directed them to a shower room and invited them to change into surgical gowns and take showers "to avoid any chance of infection". They obeyed, too anxious to fully enjoy the luxury of the copious hot water and the sweet-smelling body washes laid out for them to choose from; feeling exposed and vulnerable at discovering themselves naked in such unfamiliar surroundings. They returned a few minutes later to find the woman holding a tray with what looked like two small shot glasses. She asked them to take one each.

"This will relax your muscles. It will make you feel drowsy and will remove any anxieties," she explained. "It tastes quite pleasant."

Gabriel picked up one of the shots and examined the amber-coloured liquid closely. Isabella followed his lead and they nervously clinked the glasses.

"Cheers," they said simultaneously, before downing the medicine in one gulp. It tasted bitter but no worse than a shot in a bar. They both winced and laughed, staring into each other's eyes as their surroundings softened and faded out of focus.

Two nurses had appeared beside them and helped them to lie on the tables. They were both happy to co-operate. All the previous fears had drained away. They felt ready for sleep, and in less than a minute both had succumbed to the temptation.

When they woke up a few minutes later they could not tell how long they had been asleep. A doctor was also in the room, but he did not signify that he was aware of their return to consciousness. He seemed cold and impersonal, in a hurry to write up his notes and stick labels on small pots of clear liquid. Gabriel tried to sit up and grimaced this time from a pain in his chest, somewhere close to his heart. He looked down and saw a gauze pad taped over the site of his pain. He glanced across at Isabella who was examining an identical patch on her breastbone, just above her perfectly shaped left breast. He felt a tiny surge of jealousy at the thought that the doctor had been able to see and touch Isabella's soft breasts while he had been asleep and unable to protect her. Small patches of blood were soaking into the centre of both pads from whatever wounds lay beneath them. The doctor glanced over and barked an instruction to the nurses.

"Give them painkillers and let them rest for a couple of hours. They will be fine after that." He turned to Isabella and Gabriel. "Drink plenty of fluids."

He left the room without glancing back and the nurses busied themselves carrying out his instructions. Gabriel was grateful to be told to lie back down. He wanted to spend as much time as possible resting on the bed, being cared for by the nurses, before he had to pull on his old clothes and go back out into the heat to resume the struggles of the street. He reached his hand out towards Isabella and she gave his fingers a reassuring squeeze as they both drifted back into a half sleep.

The following day they both faintly remembered being asked to sign lots of papers before they were given two envelopes full of money, helped back down to the street and sent on their way. The same eyes that had seen them leave the favela watched from the shadows as they made their way slowly back up through the narrow streets.

Chapter Two

If the caterers had foreseen the commotion, they would undoubtedly have arranged things differently. As it was, their only hope was to make a frantic attempt at damage limitation. If Carole Madison had foreseen it, she would also have taken steps to reduce the carnage, possibly by forbidding it from happening in the first place. In fact, the only person who could have foreseen it was Larry McMahon himself and he obviously didn't care, taking enormous pleasure from garnering so much attention for his own arrival at the party by temporarily destroying it.

As the wind from his helicopter's blades ripped the starched tablecloths and napkins from the tables and sent the pale grey sunshades spinning across the lawn, causing the other guests to run for cover and the Mexican waiters and waitresses to brave the gale as they desperately flung themselves across tables to pin down anything breakable, no one was left in any doubt that Larry had "arrived" in every sense of the word.

Carole prided herself on her ability to remain calm in any social crisis, but that bright, sunny afternoon she was unable to stop her irritation from showing as Larry jumped out of the helicopter and strode across the lawn, arms extended to embrace her and her husband, obviously confident that they would be thrilled to welcome him.

"You are such a show-off, Larry," she said as she hugged him back. "Look at the mess. Couldn't you have driven here like everyone else?"

"I wouldn't want to be late for one of your famous Oakdale parties," he replied, surveying the scene of devastation without a hint of embarrassment, an arm round each of their shoulders as he beamed out at the assembled crowd. "Can any of you guys believe that this dude is sixty-five years old? I'm telling you, he doesn't look a day over forty – and he doesn't even use a surgeon."

He laughed loudly at his own joke. Everyone knew Larry must have had a lot of work done just before his second wedding to Serena, a woman not much older than Geoff and Carole's daughter, Julia, who was standing nearby with a group of friends, watching the mortified look on her father's face as his oldest friend made him the centre of attention.

Whoever had done the work on Larry's face must have been good because he looked at least twenty years younger than his friend, although to Julia's eyes her father seemed by far the better looking of the two. There was something about Larry that had always made her uneasy, even when she was a child. She never had cause to complain about him to her parents because he had never actually touched her inappropriately, but she had always felt that the potential for evil lurked just beneath the surface. She hid her distaste well as she knew her father was fond of his old friend and she would never have wanted to displease her father.

"Happy birthday, big guy," Larry boomed, and several people raised their glasses as if to toast their host.

"No, please," Geoff protested, "this isn't a party for me. This is a send-off for Julia."

"Sure." Larry spotted Julia and redirected his hug, almost sweeping her off her feet. "It's a great thing that you're doing, Julia, a really great thing. Look how beautiful she is" – he was addressing the crowd again – "this girl could have been one of the top models in the world and she has chosen to do good work – as well as helping her old father in his business. She's an angel and an example to us all."

"Jesus, Larry." Julia laughed uncomfortably, returning the hug and then struggling in vain to wriggle free of the bear-like grip. "It was a summer job for a few months before going to Yale. It was like ten years ago. When are you ever going to get over it?"

"My god-daughter becoming a top model in Paris is something I'm going to be boasting about for the rest of my life," he said, grabbing a glass from a passing waiter with his free hand and surveying the watching crowd with obvious satisfaction. There were few things Larry enjoyed more than being the centre of stage.

"Julia has achieved a lot more impressive things since then, Larry," Carole chided gently, giving her daughter a proud look.

"Of course, of course," Larry agreed, "one of the best brains in the company, almost as good as her old dad!" He finally released Julia to slap Geoff heartily on the back. Geoff knew Larry well enough to brace himself in advance for the impact and to avoid being knocked off his feet. "Not sure how you are going to manage without her."

"Hopefully he's going to recruit some new senior partners," Carole said, spotting an opportunity to advance her own agenda, "and start to take things easy. Maybe we'll even get to do that European trip he has been promising me for so long."

"Julia's only going to be gone for a year," Geoff said, turning pleading eyes onto his daughter. "I think I can hold on that long."

"Of course you can," Larry boomed. "Safest pair of hands in the business. It's way too soon to be thinking about things like retirement."

Julia squeezed her father's arm reassuringly as other people came up to talk to Larry, distracting him from his performing mode, and returned to the friends she had been talking to before the helicopter scattered them. They all drifted down towards the beach at the end of the garden. To be at a garden party on a sunny Sunday afternoon in the affluent suburb of Bloomsbury was an opportunity none of her friends would have wanted to miss. Not all of them could understand why Julia had decided to jump off the career ladder in her father's law firm to work for a charity in Rio for a year, but all of them had to grudgingly admit that they admired her for it.

Geoff was something of a legend among young corporate lawyers and part of the legend was that he was painfully shy and reclusive. Carole had had to work hard to talk him into throwing this party on his birthday and had only managed to persuade him by saying it was a send-off for Julia. Geoff would do anything for his daughter, a fact that Carole was more than happy to exploit when necessary.

About a hundred people were now wandering around the lawns and sitting beneath the mature trees which screened the garden from prying eyes. Those who had known Geoff a long time also knew that if they were invited to Oakdale they would be drinking some excellent wines. Wine was his passion and he took an interest in every bottle in his extensive cellar, either because he had been given it as a gift or because he had purchased it based on advice from a friend whose judgement he trusted on such matters. He kept notes on each wine, sometimes a review he had found, other times just a record of when he had purchased it and why. He had spreadsheets drawn up years into the future which listed when he planned to open each vintage to catch it at its peak moment. He was never happier than when regaling his guests with the backstories as they tasted his favourites. Being able to impart facts and tell stories helped him through social exchanges that he might otherwise find difficult. He was particularly loyal to American wines and that day the red he had chosen was a Chalk Hill 2005 Cabernet Sauvignon, the white was a 2008 Chablis.

*****

Julia had lived in Oakdale all her life until moving temporarily into her own apartment in Manhattan, and it had come to symbolise for her the stability and security of her parents' marriage and the whole family's roots in the past. It was a seven-bedroom house and had been standing in its stately two acres of land for close to two centuries. In recent years, the private beach had been like a weekend sanctuary for her from the high-pressure world of corporate law and the seemingly endless meetings with clients in Wall Street offices where everyone appeared to be enduring too much pressure to be comfortable in their own skins.

Every morning that Julia was back at home, she was woken by the gentle cooing of the pigeons in the giant trees. She would lie in bed watching the squirrels leaping from branch to branch without a care in the world and felt grateful for everything she had been born to. She knew from listening to her friends talking about their career and marriage worries that it made planning for the future much easier when you had such firm roots in the past and a family that you knew would always be there for you when you needed them.

It sometimes felt as if the house, and the trees that surrounded it, contained wisdom of their own, attained simply by standing still for so long, watching everything that happened both inside and outside the sturdy walls. There is something about an old property: it is wise because it has had time to learn, knowing its place and its role, and commanding respect simply for existing, enduring and slowly maturing.

Julia had always loved that throughout her youth her parents had encouraged her to invite her friends to Oakdale, and she was proud that her friends always wanted to come. They could sit fifty yards out in the garden in total privacy, chatting about careers, college and boyfriends, both current and past. Their laughter and conversations would be carried away in the breeze and were indecipherable by the time they reached the house. They called it the "fifty-yard line". Not that they would have minded Carole and Geoff overhearing anything they might have been saying. Unlike most other people's parents, they never seemed to judge and they never seemed to be shocked by anything they overheard. They didn't even offer advice unless they were asked. Most of the time they pretended not to hear, although Julia knew that they took in everything. Her parents seemed to her to be as wise as the trees and the house itself. As she watched Larry working the crowd with his exaggerated high spirits and fake bonhomie, she was deeply grateful that he was only her godfather and not her father.

She knew that her father felt the same way about Oakdale as she did. He adored the place and she often saw him wandering through the gardens after dinner, nursing a glass of wine and reflecting calmly on the happenings of the day. It was the contemplative side of his nature that she loved so much. Most of the men she met through business were more like Larry – or at least aspired to be like Larry. They were loud and overconfident and strove to dominate any group they were in. Geoff wasn't like that, but all those high-achieving alpha types respected him for his experience and calm good sense. Many of her friends also had reason to be grateful to Geoff for his sage advice when they were trying to decide which colleges to attend and which firms to apply to for internships. He always had time to dispense advice to anyone who might ask for it, and if he promised to give them a reference or make a phone call on their behalf, he always kept his word.

Many of the guests that day were neighbours that Geoff and Carole had known ever since they bought the house thirty years before. A few of them were young Porsche-driving dot-commers and new Wall Street stars, but most were the recipients of second-and-third-generation wealth. It was the company of these people that Carole and Geoff were most comfortable in because they could be trusted to provide privacy and discretion. In what felt like an increasingly unsafe world it was good to feel that there were some people you could always rely on.

Being a naturally cautious man, Geoff had been reluctant to give his blessing to the idea of Julia walking away from her career for a whole year and going to work in an area as famously dangerous as the favelas of Rio. Carole had lobbied hard on her daughter's behalf. If she had thought that her husband could manage without her, she would happily have volunteered to go with Julia. For many years, since retiring from her medical practice, she had put all her considerable energies into charity work and had come to the conclusion that the whole system for eradicating poverty needed to be rethought.

"A billion or more people are still poor after decades of development aid interventions," she would argue whenever she had an audience for the subject, "so obviously the current system does not work. We have to think much more radically about how to help those at the bottom of the financial food chain to earn more and to improve their standards of living."

Julia had done some pro bono work after graduation but, like her mother, she now wanted to make a contribution at a more strategic level. The place that had affected her most during her travels had been Rio and she had always harboured a dream of going back one day and making a serious difference.

"You took a year's sabbatical when you were my age," she had reminded her father when he protested at the impracticality of her plan.

"That was a long time ago," he replied, "and rural Zambia is a very different situation to the favelas of Rio. Rio's poverty has fostered a culture of violence and drugs – personal safety is a big issue. Zambia was different. The big issues there were access to food and water. I was also very different to you when I went there. I didn't go to solve the problems of the world. I went as a simple volunteer to better understand what was happening on the ground in one of the poorest regions of the world. Also, and you may not like to hear it, women are more vulnerable in these situations than men."

"I don't know that that is true, Dad," she argued. "It's nearly always young men who kill each other in knife fights. And it's mostly men who run the crime."

"A young woman travelling on her own is always going to be vulnerable," he insisted. "It's a fact of life and you know it."

"You have to trust me, Dad. I'm an adult."

"Of course I trust you," Geoff said. "You know perfectly well I do. It's everyone else I don't trust."

They had both laughed, knowing that neither of them would change the mind of the other. Their laughter had relieved the tension. Julia did know perfectly well how proud her father was of her and that he would never ultimately stand in her way. He would always back her, whatever she might choose to do and whatever his personal reservations might be. Both Geoff and Carole knew that Julia had made up her mind and would have gone anyway, with or without their approval.

Julia had two older brothers, but neither of them had chosen to go into law, which was a disappointment to their father even though he never said anything, and even though each had become successful in their own sphere. Matt, an accountant, was rising through the ranks in Bank of America and it seemed to his sister that his conversation consisted solely of subjects like collateral, credit swaps, derivatives and futures. Doug had chosen to go into real estate and seemed to complain constantly, both in the good years and the bad. From the look of his home and the cars he drove, however, he seemed to Julia to be doing OK. All three children had learned, from watching their father, the values of a strong work ethic and of pursuing the highest levels of professionalism in whatever they chose to do.

It was her brothers' children, as well as some of the neighbours' grandchildren, who now ran joyfully around the lawns.

"Children are the same all over the world, aren't they?" her father had said to her earlier in the afternoon. "Rich or poor, they don't care. They just accept what life hands out to them and enjoy every moment for itself. We could learn a lot from them."

Julia knew that he was wondering whether she would soon be adding to the total of grandchildren in the family but was too diplomatic to ask her such personal questions. Her brothers suffered from no such inhibitions.

"Still no boyfriend, then?" Doug had teased her.

"Still frightening them all off with your big brain?" his brother joined in.

"You can both flip right off," she said laughing. "Having grown up with you two I'm in no hurry to clutter my life up with another deadbeat guy!"

"Tick tock, tick tock…" Doug joked. "Can you hear that, Matt?"

"Yes, I can, Doug," his brother replied. "Would that be our little sister's biological clock ticking away?"

"I think it could be, Matt."

"I'm only twenty-nine, for heaven's sake," she said, giving them both a shove with her shoulders. "Still virtually a child."

Her brothers weren't the only ones to comment on her continuing single status and Julia had to struggle not to show her annoyance at the repeated astonishment well-meaning friends of her parents expressed that "such a beautiful girl" couldn't find a man.

Larry was shouting again, summoning everyone to gather around him, obviously feeling that it fell to him to make a speech on behalf of all there. No one questioned why he might believe it was his place to dominate the party. They knew he was virtually one of the Madison family. All the adults on the lawn also knew that he owned and ran the Yokadus Corporation, one of the biggest international pharmaceutical and health groups. His high profile in the corporate world added to the interest people paid to anything he might have to say. However bombastic his delivery might be, it was obvious to those watching that he had a deep affection for Geoff and his family.

"OK," he shouted, waving his wine glass in the air, "listen up, everyone. There's something you all need to know." It was a few seconds before they had finished their conversations and turned their full attention to the billionaire, who took the opportunity to wrap his arm vigorously around Geoff's neck. Geoff's discomfort at having so much attention focused in his direction was clear to see.

"What you all need to know," Larry continued once he was assured of everyone's focus, "is just how much I love this guy...and Carole and the kids. They are like my family. In fact,

I think I love them more than my own family." There was a nervous ripple of laughter. Everyone knew how acrimonious his divorce had been and how young his new wife was. It was also painfully obvious that she had chosen not to accompany him to the party. "This guy has been with me every step of the way ever since the day we met on the football field as kids. I have gone on kicking his ass every day of his life since that first game." Several people averted their eyes, not sure if he was joking or boasting. Geoff disentangled himself from Larry's grip and shook his head to the crowd.

"That's what he likes to think," he said, "but I ask you, who's been paying who a monthly retainer for the last thirty years?"

Another relieved ripple of laughter passed through the crowd. Larry might look twenty years younger than Geoff with his judicious use of Botox, hair dye, surgery and whatever else was available, but it was Geoff who exuded the greater aura of wisdom and quiet self-assurance, regardless of any grey hairs on his head or lines in his handsome face. Their host, it seemed, emboldened by a couple of glasses of wine, was willing to play along with the joke, pretending there was a rivalry between them. Those who understood the history of Yokadus knew that Larry would never have been able to build the company to the size it was without Geoff's sage advice and legal skills. They also knew that Larry was not Geoff's only client, even if he was the oldest and biggest. If Yokadus took their business somewhere else, Geoff's firm would suffer some temporary pain, but it would certainly survive. How long Yokadus would survive without Geoff's steadying and restraining hand was less certain.

Larry had always been a risk-taker and there had been many instances when he had wanted to leap into a new business area before the patents were safely secured or before due diligence had been undertaken. Larry might produce all the noise and bluster but whenever it came to boardroom showdowns, it had always been Geoff's calm approach and mastery of the fine details of the law that had won the day.

"Today we're celebrating his sixty-fifth birthday—"

"No, we're not," Geoff said, his expression exasperated while his voice was resigned to the fact that his friend was uncontrollable.

"Sure we are," Larry crashed on, unconcerned by his friend's obvious discomfort. "Isn't that right?" Now he was addressing the crowd and a few brave souls raised their voices in agreement and their glasses in a toast to their host.

"Seriously," Larry continued, and those closest to him could see that his eyes were watering with real emotion, "this guy has been like an older brother to me and he better not be thinking about retiring!"

"We'll see about that," Carole chipped in and everyone laughed, knowing how long she had been lobbying her husband to step back from the business and spend more time with her.

"Love you like a sister, Carole," Larry joked, giving her a noisy kiss on the cheek. "You are like the annoying baby sister I never had." There was more laughter and a few cheers.

"OK, ladies and gentlemen" – Geoff stepped forward – "take no notice of Larry. He's been drinking my wine for half an hour and he's a babbling drunk already! The real reason we're here is to wish Julia bon voyage. I know I'm biased, but I think you all know what a great person she is—"

"Hear, hear—" a couple of voices chimed in.

"And many of you know just how indispensable she has become to the practice. One day, whatever Larry might say, I will be retiring—"

"Hear, hear." Carole raised her glass.

"And I very much hope I will be handing the practice over to Julia. That has always been my dream."

Doug and Matt exchanged glances but said nothing. They were both aware that their father would have loved it if all three of his children had followed him into the family firm. They were grateful to Julia for taking at least some of the pressure off them.

"But of course there is too much of Carole's DNA in this girl for her to be happy just to take over one of the best corporate law practices in New York," Geoff continued. "She also wants to save the world. It's a big job, but somebody's got to do it and to be honest I can't think of anyone better qualified. Not only does she have one of the best legal brains I've ever come across, she also has one of the kindest hearts. So ignore Larry and all his birthday nonsense, just join me in raising your glasses and wishing Julia bon voyage and… please…a speedy return from the favelas of Rio."

"Julia!" they all cried out in unison, raising their glasses and then applauding.

The group of friends surrounding Julia raised their glasses too, albeit with a look of sadness in their eyes.

"Cheers, favourite child," Doug joked.

"Well, not much competition really," she replied with a grin, before escaping back across the lawn with her friends to the blankets they had been sitting on before Larry had summoned them to the speeches.

"Do you think your dad will retire?" Laura, one of her Yale friends, asked.

"I don't think he would ever want to," she admitted, "but Mum can be very determined when she wants something to happen badly enough. She's worried that he'll work till he drops and they won't have any time together to do all the things she has dreamed of since they married."

"And would you want to take over the practice and become a fat-cat lawyer?" Jess, a friend from her childhood, asked. "Or will you find your vocation in the slums of the developing world?"

"Does it have to be an either or?" Julia asked. "Can't a person do good deeds in the world and good legal work?"

"Hail, superwoman," Laura, who had given up work when she married a young dot-com billionaire, said, and raised her glass and drained it in one.

"Seriously, Jules," Olivia, her oldest friend asked, "if you had to choose?"

"Ask me again in a year," Julia replied.

"Doesn't it frighten you?" Laura asked.

"Doesn't what frighten me?"

"Losing a whole year of your career. There's already another generation of hot young lawyers snapping at your heels. Can you really afford to throw away a whole year?"

"I don't see it as throwing anything away, or wasting anything." Julia drained her glass before lying back on the blanket and closing her eyes in the hope that it would stop the endless flow of unanswerable questions. She didn't want to talk about it because it was true, she did worry that she would come back in a year and find that she had missed her chance of taking over the company from her father, but on the other hand she didn't want to get to sixty without doing anything other than be a corporate lawyer all her life. She also felt guilty to think that her father might be postponing his retirement because of her, depriving her mother of his company while they were both still young and fit enough to enjoy it. If only life wasn't so short, she thought. If only there was time to do everything you wanted to do. Bubbling underneath all these thoughts was the knowledge that she was, as her father had pointed out, putting herself in the way of danger by travelling to the slums of Rio alone. She had to bury all such thoughts immediately because there was no doubt in her mind that it was morally the right thing to do.

Larry only stayed at the party for an hour, hugging Geoff close to him one final time as the pilot restarted the helicopter's engines, drowning out the peaceful chatter of the other guests once again.

"We're gonna be talking tomorrow," Larry shouted into Geoff's ear over the noise. "We've had a breakthrough. We need you to make the whole thing watertight. It's going to be the biggest thing since penicillin, trust me."

"I look forward to it," Geoff said with an ironic grin. He was used to Larry's boundless optimism and hyperbole about every new product. "You know where to find me."

"Seriously, Geoff, this is the big one." Larry gave him one more squeeze before running to the helicopter. As it rose into the air, the wind from the rotors swept once more through the tables and lifted the dresses of the women. Geoff could see Larry waving and laughing from inside, still shamelessly delighted at the chaos he was causing. As the sound of the engine faded behind the trees, calm descended once more on the ancient garden.

Chapter Three

The following morning Geoff Madison found himself smiling as he drove to work and reflected on everything that had happened at the party, from the havoc caused by Larry's arrival to the joy with which his grandchildren had played in the sunshine. It was such a happy day that it had helped him to forget for a while how much he was going to miss having Julia around the office. Although she had assured him, before leaving for the airport that morning, that she would only be away for a year at the most, he knew there was a danger she would become so engrossed in helping people in a hands-on way that she would decide not to return to the rarefied world of corporate law.

Geoff prided himself on his record for supporting the underdogs over the years in many law courts, but he quite understood why actually getting out into the community to offer practical support would be a more attractive option to someone as young and idealistic as Julia. He wished he could suppress the fears he harboured for her personal safety. She had always taken too many risks, from when she was a small child and first started riding ponies with reckless speed to when she was travelling the world alone. So far she had been lucky but he was painfully aware that no one's luck holds out for ever.

There was, however, nothing he could do to change her nature. In the early years of his marriage, Carole had often challenged him about the need to do more to help ease poverty and less to line the pockets of people who would inevitably become billionaires, like Larry McMahon, and he knew that Julia took after her mother in as many ways as she took after him.

He had never disagreed with Carole about the rightness of any of the good work that she did, but he had always robustly defended the work that he did for his clients. Many of them, like Larry, were in the pharmaceutical and healthcare industries. Their discoveries and the products that resulted from them had helped millions of people. They had eased a lot of people's pain and extended a lot of lives. Other clients had grown wealthy through working in the biotechnology fields, developing ways to increase food production through genetic modification, allowing the world's population to grow and virtually eradicating starvation in many countries. Things weren't always as black and white as the charity spokespeople and campaigners against poverty made out.

He was as aware as anyone that genetic modification was a controversial area, but no one could argue with the figures. Life expectancy had risen all round the world and fewer people went to bed at night hungry, even in the least developed countries, despite predictions in the past that a sharply growing global population would inevitably lead to widespread starvation. He had helped those good things to happen and he was proud of that. None of those developments would be possible, he told himself, if the scientists and the manufacturers had not been able to protect their patents. They would not be able to afford to do the research if they were not able to safeguard their investments and exploit their discoveries in the marketplace.

He had often had to argue his case at dinner parties with Carole and her fellow charity workers and he had become adept at it. At the back of his mind, however, he was always aware that many of his clients, including Larry, made obscene profits while many of the people who they were selling products to at inflated prices were still living in abject poverty, even though their lifespans might have been extended.

Julia had one of the best legal minds he had ever come across, but she also had a social conscience which might very easily pull her away from the career path he had planned for her. He knew that neither Doug nor Matt had any interest in keeping the family business going. If it was to survive another generation, it was going to be down to Julia to shoulder the burden. This year's break might even make her a better lawyer when she came back, giving her first-hand insights into issues that someone who never left downtown Manhattan, unless it was to travel home to the Upper East Side, was ever going to be able to fully appreciate. All these arguments had been going round in his head in the last few weeks as he tried to put a positive spin on Julia's decision. The bottom line, however, was that he was going to miss her, and also that he was inordinately proud of her.

"Just let her get it out of her system," Carole had advised him when he had confided his fears to her late one night.

"But what if she falls in love with some Brazilian guy and decides to stay there. Do you want your grandchildren to be living that far away?"

"She could just as easily meet a Brazilian in Manhattan, or an Australian or a Russian, for that matter," Carole pointed out. "If you try to stop her going, you run the risk of driving her away from us anyway."

It was good advice, he knew that, but he was still going to miss her. In the few years she had been working at Madison and Partners he had got used to walking down the corridor after most of the others had gone home for the night, sinking into one of the leather sofas in Julia's office and letting her pour him a drink as they sat together, talking over the day's events.

He was dressed immaculately for work, as always. He had used the same tailor and the same shoemaker for the last twenty years – neither had ever let him down, understanding exactly the sort of quality and style the managing partner of the most prestigious intellectual property and patent attorney office in New York needed. Unlike many people in his line of business, Geoff had never been comfortable flaunting his wealth, but he still took a great deal of pride in his appearance. His favoured style was timeless, understated elegance.

The offices of Madison and Partners also reflected his personal style, providing an oasis of calm and professionalism to soothe the minds of those who worked there and to give confidence to clients who brought their worries and problems to his door. Much of the mahogany and leather furniture had not been replaced in fifty years but it shone with the same well-tended polish as when it was first built by European craftsmen. It was as if time had stood still since the day Geoff's grandfather had retired and his father had taken over. Visitors were served tea or coffee in fine china cups on sterling-silver flatware, and the loudest sound in reception was the ticking of the grandfather clock which always kept perfect time. The entire operation worked like the proverbial Swiss watch. Deadlines were always met and few mistakes were ever made.

Geoff found great strength in knowing that he was liked and respected in equal measure by the fifty staff members. Greed had no place at Madison and Partners and customer service had been the unspoken mantra long before the populist business gurus starting preaching and writing books about it. The whole New York legal system, from clients to judges, was familiar with the Madison culture. Julia had fitted in beautifully, right from when she did summer internships with Geoff while she was at Yale.

The summer when she had gone to Paris, and had accidentally fallen into modelling after being spotted at the airport by a model scout had shown her just how chaotic and cruel the outside world could be to some people, even in sophisticated First World countries, and had made her all the more appreciative of the protection her father offered both to his family and to his clients. He made everyone around him feel safe. Despite the modelling agency dangling some glamorous offers in front of her she had never gone back and had joined the family firm full time after graduating. She had seen how ruthlessly teenage models were exploited and how quickly they were cast aside as soon as they started to mature and look like adult women; the young women's professional lives ended before most other people's had even begun. She had no intention of letting that happen to her.

Walking over the familiar Persian carpets that lined the panelled corridor leading to his office from reception, Geoff noticed that someone was already working at Julia's desk with the door open. It felt strange not to see her there and he experienced a physical pang of sadness at the thought of how long it would be before she returned.

At precisely 9 a.m. his cell buzzed. It was a number he only gave to a few of his most important clients, friends or to family members. The screen informed him it was Larry calling.

"Good morning, Larry," he said.

"You are about to receive a package. It has to be handed directly to you and it is for your eyes only. If, for any reason, you are leaving the office before you have finished reading it, ensure it is in your safe. This is just for you, Geoff. Do you understand?"

"This is a bit melodramatic, Larry," Geoff said laughing, "even for you."

"Just tell me you understand."

"Of course. I understand."

Geoff hung up just as Joanne, who had been his PA for more than twenty years, tapped on the open office door and passed him a business card.

"This gentleman is outside with a package from Yokadus," she informed him, the stiffness of her posture suggesting that she disapproved of such a breach of normal etiquette. "He insists that he has to hand it to you personally."

"That's all right, Joanne," he said. "Mr McMahon just called."

Geoff glanced at the card. It simply bore the name and telephone number of Quentin Jamieson, Yokadus's chief legal officer. Geoff had dealt with the man on many occasions and still he felt he had to send in a business card to announce his arrival. He was the most formal man Geoff had ever had to deal with, which had been exactly why Larry hired him. Joanne ushered Quentin in.

"Good morning, Mr Madison," he said with what could have been a slight bow of the head.

"Hi, Q," Geoff replied, being deliberately informal and enjoying the look of distaste flickering across Quentin's face.

"Are you expecting a package from Yokadus?"

"Apparently so."

"Please sign here."

Geoff signed the proffered form and Quentin left with the smallest of nods to Joanne as he passed her in the doorway. The package was tightly sealed and marked as "personal" and "for the eyes of Geoff Madison only". He sighed and dropped it on the desk. Normally paperwork from clients went through a number of junior partners' hands before it reached his desk. It was possible that he was now going to have to spend the whole day reading something that could easily have been dealt with by someone else, just because of Larry's need to make a drama out of everything.

"Here's your schedule for the day," Joanne said, placing an immaculately typed sheet of paper in front of him, just as she had every day for more than twenty years. Other partners in the business had started to receive their schedules on their phones, but Geoff and Joanne preferred to stick to the way they had always done it. There was something reassuring about holding an actual sheet of paper in your hands, and Joanne took great pride in the way she laid the day out for her boss. He scanned it while she stood quietly to one side, waiting to hear if he had any instructions for her. It was a normal day, with a lunch scheduled with one client and dinner with another. His phone buzzed again.

"Has it arrived?" Larry asked.

"Yes, Larry, it's arrived."

"Put everything else on hold until you've read it. This is serious, Geoff. It's my late birthday present to you. It's going to make us all rich."

"You are already rich, Larry," he reminded him.

"This is going to multiply everything by a factor of a million. Seriously, Geoff. Clear your diary. Read it."

"I'll do my best." He cut Larry off, mildly irritated at being pushed so hard, although not surprised.

Joanne had obviously overheard.

"You are due to lunch with Jake Phelan," she reminded him, pointing to the schedule. "I booked Joey's. You've already postponed him twice."

"Really? Twice? OK." Geoff glanced at the package and thought for a moment. "Don't change the lunch but clear the afternoon and evening for me. I'll do all my urgent calls this morning to get them out of the way."

"Yes, Mr Madison."

"And put this in the safe until this afternoon, will you?" He passed her the package.

His phone buzzed with a text as Joanne left the room. *Have you started reading yet?* Larry asked.

I'll get back to you as soon as possible, he texted back.

For the next four hours he talked to clients and signed whatever Joanne put on the desk in front of him. Every half an hour his phone would buzz with a text from Larry but he didn't bother to reply. Yokadus might be his biggest client, and Larry might be his oldest friend, but he was not Geoff's only client and nor was he his only friend. By twelve thirty Larry was simply texting ?.

*****

At one o'clock Geoff made his way out to lunch, reluctantly slipping his phone into his pocket. Joey's Bistro was always good and the staff knew exactly what he liked to eat and drink, never bothering to show him a menu. It was just one block away and the management billed directly to the firm, meaning he and his guests could get up and leave as soon as they were ready without any of the embarrassment of arguing about who was going to pay.

Jake Phelan was a young guy in a hurry and Geoff always enjoyed their lunches together. In all the years Geoff had been working with him, Jake barely seemed to have aged a day. When asked he would put it down to a strict fitness regime but Geoff didn't believe him and sometimes wondered if he had already started having plastic surgery.

Jake ran the engineering division of UTT, another conglomerate chasing Yokadus for market share in a number of sectors. He liked knowing that he shared a lawyer with Larry

McMahon, a man he looked on as a role model, although he would never have admitted that to anyone. He also liked to be seen in the right places with the right people – one of whom was Geoff Madison. Like Larry, Jake was a workaholic and was always looking for advice, contacts, pearls of wisdom and anything else that a wise old owl like Geoff could offer. Geoff knew what Jake was like, and understood exactly why he liked to meet him in public places, but he respected him nonetheless. He loved Jake's high energy and youthful exuberance, coupled with an integrity that Geoff liked to believe was deeply engrained in his genes. There had been a time when he had wondered if Jake would make good son-in-law material, but Julia had made a wry face when he once dared to suggest it while the two of them were taking a leisurely stroll along the beach at Oakdale.

"Are you kidding, Dad? The guy is married to his phone. He is the worst husband and father material ever!"

Jake had since married Lucy, a good friend of Julia's, and Geoff had heard that he had not been home for a family meal once since the end of the honeymoon. He had to admit that Julia had been right, but he still enjoyed Jake's company now and then, and he was a regular source of new business. Geoff had known Jake's father for fifteen years before he died unexpectedly young of a heart attack. It had been a tragedy and a shock to many of his peer group and contemporaries in the business world, many of whom believed that they were immortal and were shocked to find that people like them actually did die without warning. Whatever he might claim to the contrary, Jake did not seem to be any more careful with his health than his father had been, despite the doctors warning him that he was genetically likely to meet the same fate. Geoff did not intend to ruin the atmosphere by lecturing the younger man on his lifestyle as he watched him tucking into a mountain of fries, especially as Jake seemed to look younger and fitter every time he saw him.

One of the secrets of Geoff's success, apart from his legal skills and despite his diffidence, was his ability to network with the best business minds in New York. Throughout the lunch Jake kept talking about his many plans, dispensing valuable nuggets of business intelligence without even realising, often seeming as guileless as a man half his age, but Geoff was only half listening, aware that his phone was buzzing every ten minutes in his pocket. No doubt someone had tipped Larry off that he had left the building for lunch and he was eager to corral him back to his desk. The harder Larry pushed the more Geoff felt inclined to take his time, if only to show that he refused to be bullied by his old friend.

Jake's phone, which lay face up on the table beside his plate, was going off even more frequently but he seemed to be able to take in whatever the messages were telling him from the corner of his eye without breaking his train of thought or interrupting the outpouring of ideas that he wanted to share.

Exercising supreme self-control, Geoff did not pull his phone out of his pocket until he was back at his desk an hour and a half later. As he had suspected, every single missed call and text was from Larry. He switched it off entirely and asked Joanne to bring the Yokadus package through and hold all his calls until further notice.

Joanne placed a pot of black coffee and the package on the desk and Geoff found himself staring at it for some time after she had left the room, quietly closing the door behind her. Although he was used to Larry being wildly over-optimistic about new products and ideas, and although he was used to him wanting everything done immediately, the bombardment of calls and texts that had been coming all morning was unusually intense. Larry was, after all, a busy man, and he had obviously spent the whole morning thinking of nothing else which suggested this was something he felt deeply and personally involved with. Geoff had been working with Larry for long enough to know that at least half of his flights of enthusiasm came to nothing, while the other half would often fulfil all his predictions for game-changing profit earners. Whichever category this new idea fell into, it was certain to involve Madison and Partners in a great deal of work, which would undoubtedly prove profitable in monetary terms. Given all that, Geoff couldn't quite explain why he felt a slight reluctance to open the parcel and release the genie from its bottle.

"It's just Larry's usual hype," he told himself. "Don't allow it to affect your judgement. Just do your job, as you always have done."

Pouring a cup of coffee, he slit open the parcel with the ivory-handled paperknife he had inherited from his grandfather, the founder of the company and the man who had first laid out the ethical rules by which it ran. He pulled out the papers and started reading, suddenly riveted to his seat and not moving as the coffee grew cold in the bone china cup beside him.

The coffee was still sitting, untouched, when he stopped reading three hours later and sat back in his chair, aware of how stiff his shoulders had become from staying in the same rigid position, his only movement the turning of the pages. He stood up and stretched before pressing the button on the desk phone to talk to Joanne.

"Any calls?" he asked.

"Mr McMahon is waiting to see you." Her voice sounded tense and he could imagine how hard she must have had to fight to keep Larry from bursting in and disturbing him.

"Really?"

"He's very insistent that you see him. Shall I show him in?"

Before Geoff could answer the door burst open and Larry exploded into the room. "At last!" he roared. "I thought you must have had a stroke or something. I told her she needed to check, you could have been lying dead on the carpet – she's one tough cookie."

Joanne was standing behind him, looking to Geoff for instructions.

"Thank you, Joanne," Geoff said, "and I apologise for Mr McMahon's rudeness."

"What?" Larry looked puzzled for a moment, entirely unaware that he might have caused any offence, as if he had only just noticed Joanne was there. "Sure. Yeah. Whatever. Can you give us a moment?"

Geoff nodded at Joanne and she withdrew, closing the door behind her, her usual air of tranquillity restored and the irritation that had built up over the last hour of having Larry pacing up and down in front of her desk suppressed. Neither man sat down; Larry still pacing and Geoff still trying to loosen up his shoulders and spine.

"Well, what do you think? It's serious, it's real, and we've done it. This is going to change the world, right?"

"I can see the potential, obviously." Geoff spoke deliberately slowly, determined to calm Larry down. "But have you thought through the ethical dimensions?"

"What do you mean?" Larry looked genuinely shocked. "This is the biggest opportunity ever to transfer wealth to those who need it most. This finally gives the poorest people in the world something to sell. And the richest people will be willing to pay whatever they are asked for. This is the biggest revolution ever! It will make communism look like..." He flailed his arms wildly, unable to come up with a metaphor that would adequately illustrate how irrelevant communism would seem as a method of wealth distribution compared to what Yokadus was about to achieve. "The implications are bigger than the agricultural revolution, the Industrial Revolution and the information revolution all rolled together."

"I understand all that..." Geoff said, still playing for time as he tried to work out what he truly thought about everything he had just read, "...but my question still stands: have you thought through all the ethical dimensions?"

"Yes!" Larry shouted. "Of course we have. Can you imagine how long we have been working on this? We have covered everything. I wasn't going to come to you until the whole thing was ready to roll out. Now I need you to make sure we are protected."

"How far are you away from doing trials on humans, Larry?'

Larry took a deep breath as if aware that he needed to calm down. "About one year after patenting – then we go to market. We will have a ready-made market of buyers and sellers from day one. It works at both ends."

That didn't answer the question Geoff had asked but he decided not to pursue it while Larry was in such an agitated state. "I need time to think, Larry. I can't be railroaded into this. It needs to be done properly."

"Why do you think I've come to you?" Larry grinned and put his arm round his friend's stiff shoulders. "You are the best man in the world to dot all the i's and cross all the t's. You have got to make this totally watertight. This is for the kids, Geoff, not for the likes of you and me. This is for those beautiful grandchildren of yours – and for the ones that haven't even been born yet. This is going to make the future work for everyone. We're creating a quantum leap for mankind, a golden age."

Geoff felt as if his brain was in overload. He understood the proposition at a macro level, but the ramifications of Larry's plan for the human race were so enormous he couldn't begin to compute them all in his mind while Larry was putting him under so much pressure.

"Leave it with me, Larry. I'll get back to you."

"That's it?"

"I need time to think and to study the papers again before I can come up with any sensible suggestions. You don't have to keep ringing me. I promise I will contact you as soon as I have something useful to say."

"Jesus!" Larry stormed towards the door. "Typical fucking lawyer. If I didn't love you like a brother, I'd punch you on the nose!"

"Yeah, yeah," Geoff said laughing, "whatever."

"I'm serious, Geoff," Larry snarled, swinging angrily back round and lunging across the room as if about to throw a punch. "Don't let me down here. I'm warning you. This is important to me and I will do whatever I have to do to make it happen. Don't underestimate what I'm capable of!"

"All right, Larry." Geoff held up his hand, aware that he had tested Larry's temper too far. "I've got the message. There is no need for threats."

Larry stamped out of the room and for a second Geoff felt a chill pass through his entire body. He knew exactly what Larry was capable of and he was deeply uncomfortable about being threatened so blatantly.

Chapter Four

Julia had never been able to shake herself clear of the memories imprinted by her first trip to Rio more than ten years earlier. That time she had been a tourist, covering as much of South America as she could manage in two months on a variety of buses. She had terrified her parents with her fearless independence but impressed them at the same time with her courage and her obvious hunger to learn about people very different to any she had ever met during her privileged childhood.

The image that haunted her most from that trip was taking a Rio tour bus up Corcovado to visit Cristo Redentor, the art deco statue of Jesus Christ, and staring out at the galvanised roofs of the tiny shacks crammed into the hills below, all shimmering in the heat, simultaneously beautiful and awful. She remembered the ragged dogs everywhere, children running around the unmade roads in their bare feet and torn clothes but always smiling and shouting happily to one another and to any adult willing to listen. She had watched as her fellow tourists took pictures through the windows of the coach and listened as they talked disapprovingly about the wealth inequality on show in the city they had come to gawp at from the comfort of their tour buses.

The bus had finally wheezed to a stop and deposited them at the top of the Corcovado Mountain, the doors hissing open to let them out of the air-conditioned interior. Julia had gazed down at the steaming city below, only half listening to the others as they chatted about where they were planning on going for dinner that evening, complained about the lack of cleanliness in their hotels and giggled about the nubile beach bodies on display on the sands of Ipanema and Copacabana.

By the time they were driving back down it was dark and there were virtually no lights in the favelas compared to the sparkle of the city below. As the others stared at their phones or dozed, Julia had her hands cupped around her eyes and was straining to see through the windows. She wished she could be living amongst the locals, experiencing life from their perspective, running with the kids, helping them to plan how to make their lives better, how to make money, stay healthy and live longer.

She hadn't felt like talking to any of the other tourists slumped around her, none of whom were close to her age anyway, because they seemed to represent a world she was eager to escape. She was sure they were all good, kind people, much like the sort of people she had grown up amongst. Their hearts were probably in the right place and no doubt they all contributed as much time and money as they felt they could to charities, but their lives were much too safe and comfortable for them to ever make any real sacrifices to help those who needed it the most. She dreaded the thought that she might end up the same as them.

Ever since that trip she had been trying to work out how it was possible that there were so many people in the world living in such complete poverty with no apparent way out. How could any decent government allow just a situation to persist in a country they had been entrusted to take care of? Why were the kids on the streets of the favelas not being looked after and educated so that they could help their families to better their lives for future generations? What could she do personally to help?

Those images had stayed with her for ten years, long after her other travel experiences had faded. All through the ten years she had followed Brazilian politics and read books by Brazilian authors until she almost felt like she had already lived in the favelas herself. Now she was back and feeling better equipped with maturity and experience to actually make a useful contribution to a world where she had so far just been a spectator. She had been tempted to stay on after her first trip, working as a volunteer for one of the many charities, but Geoff had persuaded her that there was always going to be a limited amount that she could do as an individual with no particular skill to offer.

"There are millions of well-meaning young kids who can offer what you have now," he told her when she first announced that she wanted to make a difference in the world. "You can certainly make a difference with your energy and your kindness, but unless you empower yourself with training or a skill in some way you will never be able to offer any more than a strong pair of hands and a willingness to get them dirty."

"That's more than most people are willing to do," she had protested. "How much help are you in your fancy office, helping billionaires get richer by exploiting everyone else?"

"But you could do much more if you had legal experience and expertise," he continued, not rising to the bait, remembering that he had felt just as indignant with his own father when he was her age. "You can always help with handing out food and organising shelter and work programmes, but if you are a trained lawyer you can help them to fight for their rights, give them a voice in the world and make a real difference. Do you want to help them for a few months or do you want to change their lives and the lives of their children and grandchildren for ever? The future generations are the ones who really need your help."

"How can learning about patent protection help people who can't even get clean water or access to education?"

"You need to educate yourself first so you have the tools to help them. The laws of ownership are what change everything, whether you are talking about them owning a little piece of land or a house, or an intellectual property such as a song they have written or a dress they have designed. If they want to start a small business to support themselves and their families, they need that sort of help even more. It all comes down to the same core needs. All I'm saying is, empower yourself first and then you will be in a better position to empower others."

Because her father had refused to get into an outright fight with her, and because he had not scoffed at her dreams as she knew many of her friends' parents would have done, and because she respected him more than anyone she had ever met, she had given in and continued with her education, joining the family firm as Geoff had hoped she would. All the time, however, in the back of her mind, she had been planning and preparing for the day she would arrive back in Rio, ready to do some serious work to readjust the world's injustices. It was probably the main reason she was still single, since every man she had met on the dating scene in New York seemed to be looking for a wife who would settle down and start a family with him. As soon as she told them about her dreams of returning to Rio they immediately lost interest.

She had told everyone, including herself, that she was only going to be there for a year, to make the move seem more comprehensible to anyone who didn't really understand what was going on in her head, but in her heart she had a feeling she might be embarking on her true life's work as the plane touched down once more in Rio. The knot of excitement in her stomach suggested that she was finally on the right path.

She had set the ball rolling by applying for a job with an organisation called Professional Support Group (PSG), an NGO that believed in housing its volunteers in the middle of the areas they were going to be working, making them integrate with the people who needed their help and become a genuine part of the communities they were going to be serving. She didn't necessarily believe she would spend her whole career with PSG, but they were a good place to start, giving her a base from which to learn what the local population needed and to start making contacts with people in authority, whether it was government officials, religious leaders or crime bosses. Once she had found out where she could most usefully apply her skills she would be able to lay down some serious plans for making a difference in the world. She was sure that with the right education, assistance and leadership, many of the bright-eyed children she had seen playing on the streets of the favelas could be saved before the syringes, the prisons, the brothels and the political system broke them down like they had broken down their parents and grandparents before them, reducing them to virtual nothingness in the eyes of the rest of the world.

Because she'd had to get a connecting flight via Miami, she had been travelling for a whole day. It was four o'clock in the afternoon and the sun was still burning with its relentless midday intensity as she emerged through the arrivals door at the airport. In the scrum of taxi drivers, tourist guides and family members there to pick up arriving travellers, she spotted the statuesque figure of Dr Beatriz Sanchez, who was holding up a sign with her name on it.

Beatriz, or "Bea" as everyone knew her, headed up the PSG operation in Rio and was talked about in reverential terms back at their headquarters in New York. In the eyes of many, she was close to a saint for her years of selfless work amongst some of the poorest people in the world. Just as Julia had gained a foundational training in law, Bea had been a successful paediatrician before turning her attention to improving the chances of those who would never in the normal course of their lives have access to any significant medical care.

They exchanged waves of recognition and when Julia eventually found her way through the crowd they fell naturally into a hug. Julia was impressed by the strength she could feel in Bea's muscular arms. If she was a mother with a sick child, this was a woman she would be happy to trust. Anyone watching them would never have guessed they were meeting for the first time; they looked and felt like they were already the oldest of friends even though they had only ever talked over Skype.

Because of her good posture, Bea looked surprisingly chic considering she was dressed in a loose black top and trousers. She had beautiful eyes which she accentuated with a heavy use of mascara, and she exuded an aura of authority and energy. Julia immediately felt as comfortable and safe with her as she would have been with her own mother.

"How was your flight?" Bea asked as she took one of Julia's cases and guided her towards the exit, unapologetically forcing her way through the crowd.

"Good," Julia shouted over the noise as she struggled to keep up.

"Did you sleep?"

"I wanted to, but I was too excited."

"We're excited to have you. We don't get many high-flying Manhattan lawyers down here."

"I don't know about 'high-flying'—"

"That's what they told me at HQ."

"They gave you pretty good reviews too," Julia said laughing. "I guess they really want us to get on."

"I'm sure we will."

Bea had abandoned her car carelessly on the footpath outside the terminal, traffic whizzing all around it. An official-looking sign in the back window proclaimed it was a "Military Vehicle", despite it being a battered family Toyota.

"The authorities believe that?" Julia gestured at the sign.

"They all know it's my car, but they have given up trying to bully me. Whatever they may say about me in New York, I have a reputation for being a difficult woman around here. The sign makes it easier for them to ignore the parking."

Inside the car there was a smell of stale cigarette smoke, even though Bea had the windows down so that she could easily shout at anyone who offended her in some way with their driving skills, or even in some cases their walking skills if they tried to cross the road in front of her. Once behind the wheel she drove fearlessly into the traffic, ignoring the angry honking of horns and the screech of brakes and tyres on hot tarmac, talking at full speed as she wove in and out of the lanes with her foot to the floor.

"The office is in the centre of the city, off Avenida Vieira Souto – I want to introduce you to some people there first. You'll be staying in town tonight, to give you a chance to orientate yourself, and tomorrow we'll take you to your new home in the favelas of Complexo do Alemão." She glanced across at Julia as if to gauge whether "favelas" made her nervous. "Don't worry, you'll be safe. We know people there, so you'll be OK."

"Great." Julia was genuinely enthusiastic, remembering her glimpse of life in the slums ten years ago and the urge she had felt then to get in amongst the people and make things happen. If anything she felt excitement rather than fear at the prospect. "I'm not worried."

"You will still need to keep your wits about you. These areas have been dangerous in the past but the government is investing billions of reals trying to urbanise them before the World Cup and the Olympics."

"Are they succeeding?"

"Not entirely. Understandably the drug barons who have been running these areas for generations do not like the initiative, and the atmosphere between them and the police is tense, but we have long-term plans which make a bit of short-term pain acceptable. There has been a fair bit of resistance and fighting in the streets. They are bound to keep flexing their muscles for a while in the hope of scaring the authorities away."

"You said, 'we have plans'. Who is 'we'?"

"PSG. We are involved in this urbanisation process. It's an enormous, complex project but if we don't plan out the next twenty years after the initial investment of money and time has been made, it will not have any long-lasting effect. It will all have been a waste. It's no good simply suppressing organised crime while the tourists are here and then giving up and handing the power back to them as soon as they've gone home. We need to leave something concrete there for the next generation to build on, to give them an alternative to crime, to give them some hope. This is where education comes in. The government is going to build the schools, but that doesn't mean they will continue to staff them once the international development money is no longer sloshing around. We need to identify and educate the future leaders now, while we have the opportunity, instilling the essence of international law and human rights into a whole generation in the hope that they will reject everything their parents had to accept through lack of alternatives. That is why we need people like you to educate the young people, to open their eyes to the possibilities of being in charge of their own futures."

"Makes sense," Julia said, realising that she was gripping the seat tighter than was strictly necessary as Bea hurtled on through the traffic, talking all the time, gesticulating with both hands and frequently looking across at her rather than at the road ahead.

"I'm going to step on it a bit now," Bea said breezily, "because I want to get us to the office before rush hour starts."

Julia took a deep breath and forced herself to stay calm, staring out the window at the passing scenes, trying not to let out frightened exclamations every time a collision with another car, motorbike or pedestrian looked inevitable. The city centre was exactly as she remembered it: hot, busy and noisy, the air thick with exhaust fumes. It was exhilarating to be back and she realised she felt happier than she had done for months. She had to admit that her father's advice had been good. Bea's enthusiasm for the organisation's plans chimed exactly with Geoff's warnings about getting legal experience before going back in order to be truly helpful in the long term.

Still a little dazed from the flights and the onslaught of sights and sounds from the Rio streets, Julia followed Bea into the PSG offices, leaving the car abandoned once more on a pavement with its official sign in the window. The door from the street led directly to a staircase that plunged down to a collection of basement rooms, the windows barely poking above ground level. Inside the open-plan rooms was a commotion of people shouting into phones and piles of paper spilling out of files which had been precariously stacked on top of ancient-looking computer hardware.

"Sorry," Bea said with a shrug when she saw Julia's shocked expression. "Like all NGOs we have to deal with a lot of bureaucracy and the concept of the paperless office means nothing to bureaucrats."

"You work on this equipment?" Julia ran her finger through the dust on top of a large IBM monitor.

"You want to buy us some new equipment, we won't be stopping you." A young guy in a grubby World Wildlife Fund T-shirt grinned at her from behind a nearby desk, cradling a phone under his chin. "Maybe organise a fancy fundraising dinner or something?"

Julia knew she was being teased and was disappointed to think she could be stereotyped so easily as a girl from the privileged side of the tracks. The guy had already gone back to arguing with someone on the phone before she could think of a witty retort.

"This is Julia Madison, everyone," Bea announced to the noisy room, and for a moment all eyes turned to her. "The big-shot New York lawyer I was telling you about."

"Oh" – Julia was taken by surprise – "not really that big shot…" then realised Bea was joking and no one was really listening anyway. A few of them waved vaguely in her direction before going back to whatever they'd been doing before and one or two stretched across their desks to shake her hand as she passed, following in Bea's wake. It seemed they had been expecting her, or at least weren't surprised to see her, but none of them had the time for small talk. She imagined they saw eager new recruits coming in every day, most of whom would give up and go home once they realised how tough things were.

Bea made them both a coffee and introduced her to more people than she could hope to remember from a first meeting. Once she could work out better what was going on, she would be impressed by all of them. The organisation obviously attracted smart, well-educated and eloquent people, but equally obviously they were drowning in paperwork and lacked the funds they needed to operate effectively. It occurred to her that the cheeky young man on the phone was right: if she put in a few phone calls to her mother and to Madison Partners' clients like Larry, she wouldn't have much trouble raising enough money to rent better premises and buy some decent computers and filing systems. Everyone seemed to be permanently fielding phone calls, riffling frantically through bulging files in search of an elusive piece of information, or talking to some intimidated visitor who had wandered in off the street in search of help or advice. She had a feeling, however, that no matter how much money was raised, they would always need more. It was like a giant black hole, impossible to fill.

"Take a couple of these," Bea said, chucking over a handful of T-shirts sporting the PSG logo. "Wear them all the time in the favelas. There's only two sizes, large or small."

"Really?" Julia eyed them suspiciously. She had hoped the locals would accept her as one of them, not see her as a do-gooder volunteer who would probably stay a few weeks or months and then return to the comfort of her own home in the First World. The message on the shirts seemed to contradict everything she wanted them to think about her.

"Yeah, really. Even the drug barons won't hassle an NGO volunteer too much."

Julia watched as Bea held a number of informal meetings around the office with different people. The pressure of the phones and the visitors coming through the door looking for help never seemed to let up. She felt she should be doing something herself but didn't know where to start or what was expected of her. She felt uncomfortable and out of her depth – an unusual sensation for her and one which she did not enjoy.

"You look like you're flagging," Bea said after an hour. "I'll take you to your hotel now and you can get some sleep."

The hotel was close to the office and mostly seemed to cater for business people and groups of middle-aged tourists, exactly the sort of people she wanted to steer clear of as she tried to melt into the local scene. Once in her room, however, she was happy to use the hot shower, eat a packet of free biscuits and flop onto the bed, where she fell fast asleep despite the adrenaline pumping through her system.

At 7.30 the next morning she found Bea double-parked outside the hotel with a phone clamped to her ear as she waved frantically to catch Julia's attention. The morning air was surprisingly fresh and cool.

"You slept well?" Bea asked once they were back on the road.

"A straight ten hours, thanks."

"Glad to hear it because you won't be in a bed that comfortable again for a while."

"Bring it on!" Julia said laughing.

Bea gave her a quizzical look as if trying to ascertain whether Julia was just another rich girl on an adventure or whether she was truly going to be up to the challenges she was about to have thrown at her. Julia grinned back confidently.

The journey to Alemão took two hours, even with Bea ducking and diving down one-way side streets to escape as many traffic jams as possible, and Julia felt the levels of excitement building in her system as the road started to climb the mountainside and the gleaming high-rise buildings began to sink below them. The sun had fired up for the day, ready to turn the hundreds of thousands of corrugated shacks into ovens, driving their inhabitants out into the narrow streets protected by their beautiful dark skin that Julia knew would make most of her white friends deeply jealous. The air no longer smelled of the sea, even though the Atlantic was only three miles away. Despite the stench of large-scale human marginalisation, Bea still insisted on keeping the windows open, her elbow resting casually on the sill, apparently unbothered that the sun was burning her bare forearm.

"What are you thinking?" Bea asked.

"The same thing you probably think every day when you drive through these places." Julia grinned.

"Oh, yeah, and what would that be, little Miss Mind-reader?"

"I was thinking that most of mankind lived like this a few hundred years ago. Many of us progressed but so many got left behind."

"Think it's possible to do anything about it?"

"I like to think that eventually everyone will catch up, but I know it won't happen without a concerted effort on our part."

"Our part? Who's us?"

"Everyone, I guess."

"Do you think it's possible to do it within a generation or two?"

"Well, we're the first generation able to communicate as extensively with one another as we do, so that means we're the first to really understand the full extent of the divisions in society. We see how other people live every day on television screens and social media and we're more aware."

"Does knowing they exist mean we understand them?" Bea nodded her head towards the people glowering in their direction on the street outside.

"No," Julia smiled ruefully, "of course not."

Bea had to slow down to not hit the dogs and cats that stood or lay in the shade and Julia was aware of the stares they were getting from the people loitering on the corners and outside the houses for no reason other than they had nothing else to do. Even when seen in a passing car, she guessed it would be obvious to onlookers that they were not locals.

"We seem to be the object of considerable curiosity," Julia said.

"You think because you wear a T-shirt and jeans you look like them?" Bea laughed. "Everything about you marks you out as different. Your skin, your teeth, your hair, nails, hands and clothes are all giveaways. You've eaten well every day of your life and you've been able to look after your body every day of your life. You've had a comfortable night's sleep virtually every day of your life. Every time you got a rash or a stomach ache you could go straight to a doctor or a pharmacist. They've had none of that. They can't even guess your age because their reference points are so different. You could pass for a teenager around here."

"I know a few people back home who pay good money to surgeons to be mistaken for teenagers," Julia said.

"Does it work for them?" Bea asked, lighting a cigarette as she waited for the traffic ahead to move and waving away a couple of young men who were closing in on her open window. To Julia's surprise they obeyed, merely standing and staring through the windscreen at her, whispering to one another and grinning wolfishly.

"Depends who's doing the looking and what you mean by 'work'," she replied, pretending that the young men's stares weren't unsettling her.

Bea drew up and climbed out of the car when the streets became too narrow to continue driving, tasking a couple of sly grinning boys with the job of keeping watch on the Toyota until she returned. Julia got out behind her and nodded a greeting at the boys, who smirked back before averting their eyes.

"We're here and I need caffeine," Bea said, disappearing into a nearby doorway, greeting the people standing and sitting in the small amount of shade provided by a thirsty-looking tree, which had a collection of ancient windborne plastic bags hanging from its branches like sun-bleached moss. She didn't look back to check that Julia was following.

The local PSG offices were located in a building that was proudly signed as "the shopping center", but which looked nothing like any shopping centre Julia had ever been to. The anchor tenant was a butcher and the flies swarmed over the meagre displays of meat in the dirty window. Bea led the way through a door beside the shop and up a rickety staircase to an office above. An antiquated air-conditioning unit roared from its position in the window, but the woman sitting behind the desk was still sweating profusely, chewing methodically on gum.

"This is our chief honcho for the area," Bea said curtly. "Maria Morales. She was a civil servant before she joined us.

She's great with the admin. Just love a bit of paperwork, don't you, Maria?"

"Sure" – Maria nodded without smiling or breaking her chewing motion – "who doesn't love filing?"

Maria seemed resentful and exasperated as Bea picked up some papers and flicked through them as she talked, pouring herself a coffee from a pot which was already brewed but not offering any to Julia. It seemed any status she might have had as a newly arrived guest had expired.

"Maria is going to be your guide to everything local," Bea said after a few minutes of scanning the paperwork. "I've got to get back to the centre of town, so she'll show you where you'll be living."

"Oh, sure" – Maria wiped the sweat out of her eyes with the back of her arm – "because I have nothing else to do all day but be a tourist guide."

"She's got a heart of gold really," Bea assured Julia. "Just keeps it well hidden."

Maria pretended not to hear but chewed with increased ferocity.

Bea swallowed the shot of coffee in one, slapped Julia encouragingly on the back and left the office, talking into her phone as she went. Julia heard her outside, shouting abuse at some more kids who had appeared from thin air to see if there was any extra money to be squeezed out of the visitor, and challenging the ones who had been tasked with protecting the car.

"Come," Maria said, standing up and grabbing some keys as they heard Bea's car revving up outside and the farewell honk of her horn. "I'll take you now."

"Thanks," Julia said. "Sorry to be a nuisance."

She didn't like the idea that she was a burden, adding to this woman's obvious heavy workload. She looked forward to being able to lighten that load for her once she had found her way around.

A small band of curious children fell into line behind them as they emerged from the shopping centre, ignoring Maria's instructions to "piss off". Some of them seemed to be laughing at private jokes while the bolder ones tried to catch Julia's eye and ask her questions. Julia made eye contact with them as they walked, which made Maria tut disapprovingly. It was obvious that the more they were encouraged, the closer they would press and the more of them there would be. Soon it was hard to move at all. Julia realised that if she ever wanted to get anywhere on these streets, she had to keep her eyes on the ground, walk fast and ignore everyone. That thought was disappointing and the reality was unnerving. She was having to make a conscious effort not to let panic take over.

They reached a blue painted door in a shack made of grey breeze blocks and corrugated iron. Maria turned on the children like a fury, waving her arms and screaming at them to go about their own business as if dispersing a pack of feral animals. The children laughed at her tirade but stepped back a respectful distance anyway, whispering and watching as she unlocked the door and gestured for Julia to go in.

"Keep the door locked," Maria said, slamming it behind them, "and don't let anyone in. You will be safe in here."

There were sturdy bars across the window and Julia could see that the door had been reinforced to ensure the privacy of anyone locked inside. She guessed that PSG had to take a few extra precautions if they were going to ask their volunteers to live in such a vulnerable place. She would have liked to show the people outside that she trusted them by not locking herself away like this, but then it occurred to her that everyone had to protect themselves in an area with high murder rates so, in fact, by locking herself in she was living exactly like everyone else on the street.

"I'm going back to the office," Maria said. "You make yourself at home. Lock the door after me."

With that she was gone and Julia was left staring at the bare brick walls, listening to the voices, dogs and motorbikes in the street outside, and perspiring heavily in the heat. There was a single tap dripping noisily into a tin basin on one side of the room. A badly stained toilet stood behind a curtain, and an electric cooker, which looked about fifty years old, sat beside a small table and single plastic chair. Apart from that there was just a bed and a shelf. She could see curious eyes staring in through the bars of the window and drew the bits of cloth that passed for curtains before lying down on the bed to gather her thoughts and steady her breathing.

After a few minutes she decided there was no option but to get back outside and try to work out what was going on and how she was going to survive the coming weeks. Pulling on a fresh PSG T-shirt, she set out to familiarise herself with the area and buy a few basic rations for the house like coffee, biscuits and fruit. Despite her experiences earlier she found it impossible to ignore the children who crowded around her, even though they were now joined by some of their older, more dangerous-looking brothers. The older girls, it seemed, had domestic work to do and less time to spend hanging out on the streets looking for interesting distractions like an attractive stranger moving into their midst. Being the centre of so much attention was simultaneously exciting and frightening. The small kids were open in their questioning and brazen in asking for money or for her to buy them things. The older boys were more reserved, watching her through hooded eyes with half-amused smiles on their lips, staring at her body, weighing her up and no doubt scoring her in their heads.

The afternoon passed slowly. She wondered if Maria expected her to come back to the office or whether Bea would show up or ring with instructions for what she was supposed to do, but no one came and her phone remained silent. By the time darkness fell she found herself sitting alone in the room, which was already beginning to feel a little like home compared to the chaotic world outside its doors, feeling grateful that at least she was able to access the internet for company. There was a wire bringing electricity in through a hole in the wall, which crackled and sparked slightly threateningly but at least it allowed her to charge her phone.

Even as darkness fell there still wasn't a second's silence outside the building. As she tried to sleep she could hear motorbikes revving, people shouting, televisions blaring and dogs barking. Some of the voices were so loud and so close they sounded like they were in the room with her. Were they doing it on purpose to unsettle her, to remind her that she was an outsider and was not welcome in their world? The edginess, coupled with the heat, made it hard to sleep however still she lay. It was a very different set of sounds to New York. It took her a while to work out what was missing and then she realised: there were no sirens.

The police and ambulances do not come here.

She eventually fell asleep at about 3.30 a.m. when the area finally fell silent for two or three hours, even the dogs having had enough of the day.

When Julia's alarm went off at 8 a.m. the outside world was still eerily quiet compared to the previous night. Those with jobs in the city had already disappeared while the air was still cool and fresh from the darkness, and those without work were still asleep. The suffocating daytime smells of cooking mixed with two-stroke engine oil had not yet started to seep from the houses into the lanes and alleys.

Julia opened the door and squinted as she stepped out into the brightness. Refreshed by sleep she felt a thrill of elation pass through her at finding herself actually living in the sort of area she had been thinking about for so long. A few people were carrying water from the nearby taps and emptying buckets from the night before into makeshift sewers at the end of the lane. The women preferred to get organised early in the day before the heat built up, even though for most of them there was nothing to do and nowhere to go for the rest of the day apart from remaining still and sheltering from the heat. The sort of daily pressures that New Yorkers with jobs and material possessions put up with didn't exist here.

Her small excursions the previous afternoon had taught her that it was going to be easy to get lost between home and work. Every lane looked the same; there were no names or numbers, no signposts. It reminded her of the time she was in the rainforest, downstream of Manaus. To her, as an outsider, every tree had looked the same. In the urban forest of Alemão, it would be perfectly possible to take a wrong turn and be lost within fifty metres of your home. How would she be able to ask for directions to a house with no number in a street with no name? Who amongst the young men whose eyes were always on her would she be able to trust to help her? How would she ever know if they were guiding her home or leading her to a place where they could do what they liked and no one would ever hear her screams?

The favela was a kind of grid on the hillside. Straight ahead, looking west, she could see a communications tower about ten miles away. She counted the houses to the end of the lane from her own blue door. That would have to do as a landmark. As she set off in search of the PSG office she felt the knot of excitement tightening in her stomach. She had no idea what adventures the day might bring in this alien world.

Chapter Five

"I've stayed off your back for forty-eight fucking hours," Larry growled. "Now you need to talk to me."

He was standing in the office doorway with Joanne hovering behind, having failed to stop him barging in.

"Thank you, Joanne," Geoff said. "Come in, Larry. Do you want a coffee?"

"What I want is for you to talk to me!" Larry said as Joanne quietly closed the door behind him. "I don't understand what's got into you. You are my rock, Geoff, always have been. What's going on?"

"I don't think I can handle this one for you, Larry. I'm sorry."

"What's the matter? Are you ill? Of course you can handle it. You can handle anything! You are the best in the business, that's why I hire you!" He was pacing back and forth in front of the desk as Geoff sank back into his chair, still confident that he would be able to push the lawyer into agreeing. Larry was used to getting his own way when he really wanted something. Having had time to calm down he was now determined to keep control of his temper and resist the temptation to lift Geoff out of his chair by his perfectly tailored collar and keep butting him in the face until he saw sense.

"We have plenty of good people here. I was thinking of suggesting we call in Daniel Steinman. He'll be the one stepping into my shoes when the time comes anyway—"

"What do you mean 'when the time comes'?" Larry looked completely bemused. "So you are ill? Jesus, Geoff, just talk to me. What's the problem?"

"I'm fine, Larry, honestly, at least physically I'm fine. This just doesn't feel right to me." He gestured towards the file on his desk. "I'm not comfortable and I've got too much on my plate anyway, mostly work I'm doing for you."

"So drop everything else. Let Steinman handle everything else. This is the big one for us now – and for you. Nothing we are doing has even ten per cent of the potential of this one. This is a total game changer."

"It's not because I don't see the commercial potential, Larry. I'm not senile—"

"Well you're sure acting senile!"

"It's just that ethically I'm not happy about this whole thing."

"Ethically?" Larry fought to control the rage that was rebuilding inside him. "This will trigger the biggest transfer of wealth from the rich to the poor in the history of the planet. It's going to make immortality possible for those who want it. How can you be worried about the ethics? You should be leading the band on this one."

"It's not about the money, Larry, and you know it."

"Everything is about the money, Geoff, and you know that!" Larry was now becoming outwardly angry. "How dare you take the moral high ground and make out you're on some higher plane than the rest of us? Just get on with the job I pay you to do."

Geoff had been preparing for several days for this meeting, telling himself over and over that he mustn't allow Larry to rile him. One of them had to stay calm if their friendship was going to survive and if Larry wasn't going to storm away from Madison and Partners taking every bit of Yokadus business with him. He knew Larry would not be able to keep the temperature down for long, so it was going to have to be him who held things together.

"Daniel Steinman is the man for this," he said quietly and firmly, "really, Larry. It's too big a job for me, I'm just plain tired. Not everyone has your energy levels, not at our age."

Larry finally dropped into one of the leather armchairs on the other side of the desk from his old friend and stared at him, completely unable to take in Geoff's attitude.

"What do you mean, you're 'tired'?" he asked eventually. "What do you mean 'at our age'?"

"I've been thinking about retiring for some time," Geoff lied.

"Bullshit! OK, so let's pretend that's true and you are out of the picture. It seems stupid but let's play that pretend game for a minute. Never mind this Steinman guy, get Julia back from whatever ghetto it is she's playing Mother Teresa in. She's the one with the Madison brain – she's the one you've been training up to take over. She can handle this with you guiding her. It will set her up for life and she will understand that it is a world-changing event, even if her father is too old and too dumb – and too 'tired'."

"You know Julia well enough to know that she won't come back just because you and I tell her to. Let me talk to Daniel first, then maybe when Julia gets back next year she can work with him with a view to taking over in a year or two."

"Are you serious about this retiring thing, then?"

"Yes," Geoff said, surprising himself with the admission, "but don't say anything to anyone because I haven't talked to Carole about it yet."

"Well she won't be trying to dissuade you. It's what she's been wanting for ten years at least." Larry was calming down, realising that shouting was not going to get him what he wanted for once, searching in his head for another way forward. "But then she won't know how much you are giving up by walking away at this moment. Another couple of years and you would have more money than you would know what to do with – you would be able to go cruising round the world for the rest of eternity."

"Sounds dreadful," Geoff said laughing.

"Yeah" – Larry bared his teeth in a grin which didn't reach his eyes – "retirement would be dreadful, you're gonna hate it. Jesus, you make me feel old, Geoff."

"That's not true. You'll never be old, Larry. You'll be twenty-five till the day you die."

They both laughed but the tension hadn't gone. They might be pretending they were just two men who had known each other all their adult lives talking about their plans for the future but both knew in their hearts that their differences were about to become irreconcilable.

"OK" – Larry raised his hands – "I give up. Let's wheel Steinman in—"

"I'll talk to him tomorrow," Geoff interrupted. "I need to talk to Carole first."

"She really doesn't know about your retirement plans yet, then?" Larry laughed unkindly. "Are you seriously going to give all this up," he gestured round the office, "just because of some cockamamie ethical dilemma?"

Geoff opened his mouth to tell Larry that the meeting was over and they would talk the following day, but Larry's phone buzzed and he left the office with a cursory wave, shouting down the line at someone else. Geoff took a deep breath and picked up the internal phone to Joanne.

"See if they can fit Carole and me into the Thai restaurant this evening, please. Then ring Carole and tell her the time and that I'll be home to pick her up. Thank you."

Joanne knew exactly which restaurant he meant, having booked it for them dozens of times, usually so they could celebrate family birthdays and anniversaries. Both she and Carole were surprised by him showing such spontaneity for no particular anniversary or celebration. It wasn't even Friday, a day when Geoff sometimes did suggest they went on a date night.

"Really?" Carole said when Joanne rang to inform her. "Is there something going on that he intends to tell me about?"

"I have no idea, I'm afraid, Mrs Madison."

"Is he about to tell me he's disappearing off on some extended business trip?"

"Not that I'm aware of." Joanne always felt a little uncomfortable when Carole tried to get information out of her about her husband. "I think he just wants to spend time with you."

"That will be lovely, then," Carole said, realising that she was putting Joanne on the spot and backing off. "Thank you."

* * * * *

A few hours later Geoff and Carole were sitting opposite each other across a table. The restaurant operated like a first-class airline flight with Thai waiters and waitresses gliding between diners, speaking in low, soothing tones, creating an oasis of tranquillity.

"This is a nice surprise," Carole said once they had been seated at their favourite table. She had deliberately not asked any questions in the car, not wanting to put Geoff under any pressure, aware from his demeanour that he had something big on his mind and confident that he would share it with her once he was comfortable and ready. All her years as a practising doctor had taught her that when people had something important to tell you, they needed to choose their own moment and sometimes that involved going several times round the houses before coming to the point.

They ordered the same dishes they always had and Geoff ordered the same wine he always did. They should have been feeling completely relaxed but neither of them was. The wine was poured, they clinked glasses and sipped and then Geoff spoke.

"I'm going to retire."

"This evening is full of surprises," Carole said, taking another sip of wine to buy herself a little time to absorb the news. If she had ever imagined the moment he would make an announcement like that she would have expected to feel a rush of joy, but instead, as she looked at his tense face, she felt something else. It was a feeling that she couldn't yet identify. "When?"

"More or less immediately, but I guess it will take a month or so to tidy everything up."

"Well, I did not expect this, but it's fantastic," she said after a couple of moments of thought. Then a notion struck her. "There isn't something else I should know, is there? You're not ill, are you? You would tell me, wouldn't you?"

"No, no, I am not ill – as far as I know."

"So what caused this sudden change of heart?"

"It just feels like the right time."

He wasn't looking her directly in the eye as he talked, and every muscle in his face looked tight. She realised that he was looking thinner than usual, almost gaunt. Carole could tell there was something he wasn't telling her, but she didn't challenge him. If he really was intending to retire, she did not want to say anything that might put him off the idea.

"So, what do you plan to do now?"

"Oh, you know – we can travel, finally visit some vineyards around the world and spend time with the grandkids…"

She said nothing as the waiters and waitresses moved silently around, preparing the table for the arrival of the food, which no longer seemed particularly interesting to her. She could tell that this was not his usual sort of carefully thought-through decision. If it had been, Geoff would have planned exactly what he was going to do with the next stage of his life. He had never before made any decision that affected the family without talking it over endlessly with her and with anyone else who would be affected. He was the most cautious and unspontaneous person she had ever known, which was one of the reasons he was so successful in his practice, always checking every word of every contract before allowing clients to sign any deal. This decision, she was sure, had been forced on him in some way by someone else. She couldn't imagine it was by his colleagues at work because she knew just how valuable he was to them, being the one who brought in most of the new business and the one whose reputation set the tone for the whole firm. But if it wasn't someone from the firm, and it wasn't a health decision, what could it be?

Unable to think of anything else to say, Geoff raised his glass again. "To a great future together," he said.

Carole played along and they touched glasses once more as she watched him closely. It appeared to her that he might be holding back tears. She kept watching him as the waiters brought their food. He was avoiding her gaze, more uncomfortable than she had ever seen him before.

"Something is wrong," she said eventually when all the staff had pulled back and Geoff was busily helping her to food from the various dishes now displayed across the table. "Talk to me, Geoff."

"Nothing is wrong, except that I'm getting old and I should hang up my work boots. I thought you would be pleased. You've been nagging me to do it for long enough."

She ignored the comment, leaning forward and placing her hand on top of his. "Talk to me, Geoff," she said again, more insistently this time.

Geoff was gazing down at the centre of the table, as if mesmerised by the candlelight. Their plates of food sat in front of them, untouched. His brain felt like it was in free-float, his eyes in a daze and glassy with tears. Carole had never seen him in such a state. For so many years he had trained himself to be discreet in every detail of his life, but he knew he needed to talk, and he needed the support of Carole, his best friend, more now that ever before. After a long silence, he leaned forward, lowering his voice.

"It's Larry..." he said. "Yokadus are planning to launch a process which will change everything..."

"And there's a problem?"

"I don't know." He looked her directly in the eye. "I just don't know for sure, Carole, but it doesn't feel right."

"What is this process then?"

"I can't talk about it. It's still confidential." He gave a rueful smile, glancing around at the neighbouring tables as if expecting to see someone taking notes.

Everyone else was engrossed in their meals or whatever they were talking about. There was little chance anyone was listening in to their conversation and if they were they probably wouldn't understand what he was talking about, but the habits of a lifetime were unbreakable for Geoff. One of the first lessons his grandfather had taught him was that you never, under any circumstances, talk about clients' business to anyone else without their express permission. He could no more have gossiped in a public place about Larry and Yokadus than he could have put his hands around his beloved wife's throat and strangled her; it was simply alien to his nature. Carole knew that and knew it was pointless to try to press him to reveal Larry's secrets. She did not doubt that her husband trusted her, but being a trained doctor she understood entirely the unbreakable bond of client–patient confidentiality.

"I'm not even sure if I know how to put into words what I feel about it," he continued, "which suggests this might be my problem more than Larry's. It's too big an ethical puzzle for me to fully comprehend. I don't seem to be able to get my head round it. I need time to think about it, to get my priorities in place."

"But why do you have to retire? Why can't you just tell him you don't want to handle this one process?"

"I have some responsibility to the rest of the team at Madison's. What Larry is proposing will make the company financially safe for years. That also affects our family as the majority owners of the firm. If I don't handle Larry right, he will take all the Yokadus business to another firm."

"He's not your only client. There are plenty more. Madison and Partners is successful partly because it is known for its high ethical standards."

"You don't understand how huge a piece of business this is going to be," he said.

"We have enough money, Geoff," she said, squeezing his hand. "We can always downsize if we have to. You don't have to do anything you don't want to do."

He shook his head. "It's not just you and me, though, Carole, is it? There's the children and the grandchildren, and the others at the firm. A lot of them have been with us all their working lives. I can't deliberately wreck their futures just because of my own qualms. They have the right to decide for themselves where they stand regarding ethical matters of this nature. I'm not even sure that I'm right in my misgivings."

"Can you give me the slightest clue what this process involves?"

He shook his head. "Maybe in a few months, once all the legal groundwork has been done."

"Eat," she said, releasing his hand and gesturing at the plates in front of them, "and enjoy your wine. We're going to be just fine."

He did as she told him, and gave her a thin grateful smile, but she could see that she had not managed to put his mind at rest. She made an effort to change the subject and he played along, both of them eager to avoid unearthing too many truths too quickly. Both of them needed time to absorb the idea of change.

*****

During the following days, Carole went into deep mourning for the Geoff she had known and loved for most of her adult life. She could see that his life had been blown apart and that he was racked with self-doubt that had never troubled him before. He had always been so sure of which path was the right one to follow. Sometimes she had disagreed with the rigidity of his arguments, but she had always been able to see the logic that he had followed to reach the decisions that he did. In most cases she could understand his logic around moral and ethical questions. Sometimes she thought he had made life unnecessarily difficult for her or the children, particularly the boys, with his unbendingly high standards of behaviour, but that had been the man she had fallen in love with and who she had chosen to help her raise a family.

Now it felt like she had lost him as surely as if he had died. In her optimistic moments she told herself that he would work everything out in time and his old self-confidence and sense of moral certainty would return, but at other times she feared the doubts he was experiencing were so profound the damage was going to prove irreversible and he would lose all the spirit that had driven him to achieve so much in his life. There seemed to be nothing she could do or say to influence the outcome of his inner struggles with his conscience. She decided that all she could do was let him know she would support whatever decision he made. He had always, well nearly always, been right about everything over the years, although often he had relied on her guidance on emotional matters that fell beyond the letter of the law. This time she had no idea how to advise him.

Everyone at the office could also see the change in Geoff. He seemed unable to focus at meetings and, while not obviously irritable, he was less congenial than anyone could remember him being. His usual crystal-clear legal brain seemed to be showing signs of disarray. When they did talk about it amongst themselves some suggested that perhaps this would be a good time for him to draw back from the day-to-day stresses of the business, that perhaps his famous mental abilities were beginning to fade with age.

Most of the staff, however, had enough work of their own to occupy their minds and did not worry unduly about their boss; only Joanne truly shared Carole's reservations about his state of mind. She was also pretty sure that whatever the problem was it stemmed from Larry McMahon and the heated meetings they had had in the office, even though Geoff had not said anything to her. She had never liked Larry. She had always dealt with him with an icy politeness, but her heart always sank a little when she saw his number coming up on her phone. He was a bully and a sociopath with no redeeming charms that she was able to discern. She was well aware that Larry hardly noticed she was there at all, which was another reason she never warmed to him. She had always marvelled at the degree of professional tolerance and patience Geoff showed towards him, no matter how impatient and abusive he might become. She could see that the two men had a tight bond, no doubt based on the length of time they had been working together, and she was also aware just how much lucrative legal work Yokadus placed at Madison and Partners. Part of her, however, would have been happy to see the firm lose the Yokadus account if it meant she never had to hear the snarl of Larry's voice again.

Geoff spent a great deal of time in his office, deep in thought, pretending that he was reading papers. He wished that his father or grandfather were still alive so that he could ask them if they thought he was doing the right thing. Was it his duty as Larry's lawyer to simply execute whatever orders he was given? Or was it his duty to follow his conscience as a human being and tell Yokadus that he wanted nothing to do with their new process, thereby endangering the livelihoods of all the people he, his father and his grandfather had recruited, trained and worked alongside? Should he risk the family fortune, which had been built to give security to all the children, grandchildren and eventually great-grandchildren just because he had some qualms about a medical process which would almost certainly go ahead whether he was involved or not?

His father had taught him to be an independent thinker and never to rely on the guidance of others in matters of conscience. That said, he always welcomed his father's counsel when it was offered. Geoff Snr built the firm that his own father had created on a powerful set of principles and Geoff would have valued his views on the situation he now found himself in. But his father had passed away many years before and he was going to have to act in the hope that his actions were guided by the teachings of the man he admired so much when he was alive. Not for the first time he wished his father had been granted another decade or two of life to be a sounding board in situations exactly like this.

Geoff loved the law because there were rules and precedents to follow and argue over. There were no such rules and precedents for the ethical and spiritual questions like the ones going round and round his head now. The best he could do was pray that as he made his decisions, he would be accompanied along the way by higher powers. He felt terrified and ridiculous at the same time to even be thinking such things. How could a wealthy sixty-five-year-old man with a close family and many kind acquaintances feel so alone?

This was not where he had intended to be at the end of his illustrious career. Part of him wanted to stay and fight it out with Larry, but he could see that Larry would never be moved on this one – there was way too much money at stake and way too wide a gap between them. He simply didn't feel up to the job of challenging Larry on something so huge. Someone else would have to fight the fight on his behalf if it turned out to be necessary. But anyway, he asked himself, who was he to decide what was right and wrong? The world was evolving and perhaps this was destined to be the future whether he was part of it or not. Legislation would deal with all the moral issues. It was not his role to protect the world from Yokadus – if it needed protection at all. And maybe if Yokadus didn't own this product, the process would fall into other, even more ruthless, hands. The arguments continued to spin round and round his head.

The only person he had confided the full extent of his retirement plans to other than Carole was Daniel Steinman, but still he didn't tell him the real reason why he had made the decision. As far as Daniel was concerned it was a normal retirement plan and Geoff was telling him first because he had to brief him about Yokadus and other clients. He promised that he would not breathe a word of it to anyone else until Geoff was ready.

Geoff trusted Daniel completely. He had been one of the first people Geoff had recruited after taking over the company from his father and Daniel had never let him down. He was the obvious choice to step into Geoff's shoes and take over the day-to-day running of the partnership. Geoff had often brought him in on Yokadus business and liked the way he handled Larry, never allowing himself to be bullied but always ready to provide the best service possible. Geoff had no idea where Daniel would draw the line regarding the ethics of this particular case, but he was confident that he would be able to bring a greater degree of objectivity than he could to the decision on whether it was something that Madison and Partners should be involved with.

At his desk the following morning he asked Joanne to hold his calls and pulled out a thick piece of personally headed notepaper, uncapped the fountain pen that his grandfather had given him on his first day in the office and started writing.

Dear Larry,

As your dear friend of many years, I would like you to be one of the first to know that, as I intimated to you recently, I've decided the time is right for me to spend more time with Carole and the grandchildren, so I'm retiring just as soon as I've handed over the current cases to the best people on our team.

As I hope you know, I have been an admirer of you and everything you have achieved in building the Yokadus Corporation and that admiration will never diminish. Because of the strength of our relationship as friends, we have been able to speak candidly to one another on matters that in other professional relationships might have proved to be stumbling blocks. I feel confident that you will be able to build a similar bond with other members of the Madison team in the coming years under the leadership of Daniel Steinman, of whom I know you already have a high opinion.

My difficulty with this particular project of yours is personal to me, and I hope you can understand my action

and that this does not impact our personal relationship
in any way. I wish you well with the project.

Sincerely,
Geoff

Sealing the envelope, he asked Joanne to get a messenger to take it directly to Larry, wherever he was.

"Do you want me to type it up for you?" she asked, looking at the envelope as if it might contain a bomb.

"No," he said smiling. "It's a personal letter. No copies need to be made."

Within hours, Larry called Geoff's mobile with a tremor in his voice. It sounded like he was having trouble controlling his rage.

"This project is the biggest thing that Yokadus have ever done," he said, his voice eerily even and slow. "Time is of the essence and you choose this moment to start playing silly moral games? You are willing to blow your whole career just to make a fucking point? You think Carole is going to thank you for doing this when I'm offering you a chance to be richer than the Rockefellers ever were?"

"It's got nothing to do with money, Larry—"

"Everything is to do with money!" The rage exploded down the line as Larry ranted for several minutes, calling Geoff every name he could think of that would demonstrate how disappointed he was in his decision. Geoff waited patiently for the tirade to die down. In years gone by Larry's insults would have got to him and he might even have shouted back to shut him up. Shouting at Larry never caused any long-lasting problems and he actually seemed to enjoy being given a bit of a fight. This time Geoff's calmness and quietness on the end of the line left him with nowhere to go with his rage and it eventually petered out as suddenly as a thunderstorm. "I don't know what the hell to say to you any more," he said, and hung up.

An hour later Geoff asked Joanne to assemble the staff in the boardroom. He was tense but clear in his own mind. The atmosphere in the boardroom as he came in was light-hearted, no one having any idea what was about to happen.

"How is everyone?" he asked as he breezed in and invited them all to sit down.

"Good," came a chorus of responses followed by laughter.

"Folks," he said, "I'm throwing in the towel. I'm retiring."

He could see from their blank faces as they stared back at him that they were processing the information, working out what it might mean to their own prospects for advancement, wondering if it would damage the company. Some of them might be feeling excited at the thought of change and new chances for younger members of the team, others might be uncomfortable at the thought of such a major disruption in a system that had been working like clockwork for years. A roomful of faces were turned towards him, all expressionless. The boss had given his all; none of them could deny that. It didn't seem too early for him to bow out, nor too late either. He hadn't overstayed, and as far as any of them knew he wasn't leaving the firm at a difficult time or under any sort of cloud.

"Madison and Partners has been the leader in its field for more than sixty years," he continued, giving them all time to adjust to the announcement, and I've had the privilege of being part of its global success for forty of those years. I am a member of a team of excellent people who take great care of their clients, and I suppose you could say that we have all benefited in some way from that level of care and the resultant success. We have developed a reputation for honesty, integrity and meticulous attention to detail. I once overheard a judge say 'Don't go up against Madison'. That is perhaps the greatest accolade you can receive in the legal profession—"

"Listen" – Daniel had stepped forward and interrupted – "obviously I haven't got anything prepared for this, and I'm sure we all have plenty we want to say to you, Geoff, but just off the top of my head I want to say a big thank you for everything you and your family have done to make this such a great place to work and for making every one of us feel that we matter to you as people, not just names on pay cheques.

"I'm sure I speak for everyone here when I say that no one I know deserves a long and happy retirement more than you do, but I'm sure going to miss you and I hope that you will find some way to continue playing a role in the future of Madison and Partners even if you aren't here in the office with us every day."

"Hear, hear," several voices chimed in.

"Thank you, Daniel. I'm sure you haven't seen the back of me completely. I would also like to take some one-on-one time with each of you before I go to chat about anything that might be on your minds. Oh, and one last thing... I will be sending out an email to clients today officially announcing my retirement, but all the rest of what I've said just now is strictly confidential."

Geoff had told Joanne of his decision privately a few minutes earlier and the news hit her harder than anyone else in the office, although she held back the tears and didn't allow anyone else to see how bad she felt until she reached home that evening. Her whole working life had been spent with this one man and now it felt like he was just walking away from the relationship as if it meant nothing. She couldn't say anything to him because she knew he would be mortified if he knew how badly hurt she felt. There would be no question that she would suffer financially in any way because Geoff was always as loyal to his staff as they were to him, but she couldn't imagine that she would want to come in to the office any more if it meant working with someone else. In her heart she had already decided that if Geoff retired, she would do the same, and the thought of her working life coming to an end so unexpectedly made her feel deeply sad. She couldn't imagine what she was going to do with the empty years that now seemed to stretch ahead.

* * * * *

That night Carole phoned her children individually to inform them of their father's decision to retire. She had to repeat the announcement several times before Julia was able to take in what she was being told over a bad line.

"I thought he was going to wait till I got back," she said when she was finally sure that she had understood correctly.

"Apparently not." Carole gave a hollow laugh. "I think Larry has finally pushed him too far."

"This is good, though, Mom, right? It's what you've been wanting to happen for years."

"Yes, I guess so."

"You don't sound sure."

"I'm not sure that his heart is really in it."

"But you will be able to spend so much more time together."

"But I don't want him here with me if he's constantly wishing he was somewhere else, constantly regretting his decision."

"He just needs time to adjust. He's been doing the same thing every day for forty years, more or less. It's bound to be a wrench."

"I know. I just don't understand why he has had such a sudden change of heart. He says it's to do with something Larry asked him to do that he doesn't agree with, but I worry there might be something more serious behind it. Things happen to men in their sixties."

"If he was ill, he would tell you," Julia assured her. "You know he would. He relies on you completely for everything medical."

"Yes" – Carole didn't sound at all sure – "I suppose he would."

"He's not ill, Mom. You can put that idea right out of your mind. Whatever it is, it's not that."

"Maybe he'll talk to you," Carole said after a few moments of awkward silence. "You two always seem to be able to talk about anything."

"Don't worry, Mom," Julia said, now feeling worried herself. "I'll talk to him, but I'm sure you're worrying about nothing. It's going to be great."

Chapter Six

"Miss Morales!" The voice came out of the shadows, angry but also a little plaintive.

Julia and Maria were walking back towards the office after visiting a family where every member was suffering from malnutrition, all of them crammed into one dirty room. They had taken them food and medicine and spent several hours helping them to clean up and cook a meal. They were now walking in silence, both of them lost in their own thoughts, both of them aware that they had done no more than scratch the surface of the family's problems. Julia was feeling deeply frustrated at the thought of how little she had achieved for them and was wondering why she had bothered to train as a lawyer when there was so much other work needing done on the ground. The news of her father's decision to retire was making her wonder if she ever wanted to go back to the office again. This all seemed so much more real and urgent. She was having trouble thinking clearly and the angry growl from the shadows made her jump.

"Miss Morales!"

Maria swung round to face the man who had now stepped forward into what was left of the day's light. "Gabriel," she sighed.

Gabriel was looking intently at Julia even though it was Maria he had addressed by name. For a moment Julia's heart rate had risen, fearful that they were about to be attacked, either verbally or physically. She waited to hear what he would say next, her Portuguese just good enough to understand if she concentrated hard.

"Did you find out anything?" he asked.

"I told you I would come and find you as soon as I had something to tell you," Maria replied, sounding partly exasperated and partly sympathetic. Julia couldn't help thinking that it was unwise to talk so rudely to someone who was obviously already on edge and might at any moment produce a knife or a gun.

"Time keeps passing, Miss Morales." He tore his eyes away from Julia and stared angrily at Maria, his hands balling into fists. "You keep promising to help and doing nothing."

"I'm doing what I can, Gabriel," Maria snapped. "You are not our only case, you know."

"Pah!" Gabriel spat. "You are all the same. What about you?" He swung his gaze back to Julia and she was shocked by the sudden intensity of his stare. "Will you help us?"

Julia opened her mouth to respond but Maria stepped between them.

"Back off, Gabriel," she shouted. "I've told you I'm doing all I can!"

"My name is Gabriel." He spoke directly to Julia, as if Maria was not there, holding out his hand. His eyes looked tired again.

"Hi." Julia shook his hand and ignored the angry noises emitting from Maria's throat. "I'm Julia."

"The lawyer from New York?" he said.

"How do you know that?" Julia asked.

"We have to get back to the office. We have work to do." Maria took Julia's arm and marched her firmly away. "I will find you when I have something to tell you," she shouted back over her shoulder.

"Don't let him charm you," Maria said, once they were out of earshot.

"Who is he?"

"He's a local drug dealer who knows how to work all the angles. He's been bothering me for months with some stupid story about how his wife has been made ill by a Western pharmaceutical company."

"He doesn't look like a drug dealer," Julia said doubtfully.

"You think not?" Maria laughed without a trace of humour. "What do you think a drug dealer looks like?"

"I don't know exactly, he just didn't seem…"

"You see? Already he is charming you. He is from the favelas and he suddenly had the money to build himself a nice house and have a big wedding. How else do you think he would be able to pay for such a thing? It happens to a lot of the young guys around here. One day they're poor, coming to us for clothes or money for a meal. The next day they look all mature and smart in their new clothes, and they come swinging around where they used to live. The ordinary people don't like it. Sudden wealth is treated with deep suspicion. These guys never deal in their own area. Then they get into trouble with the big guys or the police and their lives become even more miserable, or even shorter, or both. Gabriel was a lovely young guy. Now he's playing with the sharks. He'll get eaten."

"Have you asked him where his money came from?"

"Of course. He says it was the pharmaceutical company that paid him."

"Is that what he has asked you to find out about?"

"Yes. I have tried, but no one has any idea what he is talking about. He's a guy from the streets with a vivid imagination. Don't let him fool you. There are plenty more like him and they will take up all your time with their tall tales if you let them, while their wives and children struggle on in silence. They get inside your head and convince you that their conspiracy theories are real, that everyone else is out to get them, that none of their predicament is their own fault. Ask Bea, she will tell you."

"How did he know who I was?"

"He lives by his wits. Young men like that make it their business to know everything that is going on in their area. A young woman like you arriving from America is going to be talked about."

"Young men? He didn't look like a young man to me."

"Well he is," Maria said, as if this proved her point, "but like all the others he destroyed his mind and body with drugs and became an old man overnight. Now he's looking for someone to blame: first this mythical drug company and then me. Don't let him add your name to his hate list. Don't let him inside your head."

The moment they walked back through the office doors Julia was swamped with phone calls and the voices of those who had been waiting all day to see them. She forgot all about the meeting with Gabriel, just one more person amongst the thousands who needed their help.

* * * * *

The sun fell quickly in the evenings and the favela was dark by seven thirty as Julia made her way back to her shack for the night. She had been told it was always wise to get home before dark, but she seldom made it and would often find herself walking briskly through the narrow laneways in the blackness. She actually enjoyed the sensory overload of those walks home, leaving the office with a heightened awareness, her heart beating a little faster than normal, her eyes striving to adjust to the little sheets of light escaping through the door frames, her ears catching fragments of voices, radios, televisions, scoldings, arguments and heated debates. The smells of cooking, moped engines and rotting waste matter interspersed with the occasional evening gusts of fresh air blowing in from the coast. Beneath it all there was always the exhilarating tingle of fear in the air.

She had learned to avoid the busiest intersections as they were where the greatest potential trouble gathered; groups of young guys with nothing to do and endless empty hours stretching ahead, who would shout out to her and sometimes follow her for a few metres, making lewd suggestions, trying to catch her attention. She had disciplined herself to ignore them and just keep walking until she reached the invisible edges of their territory, knowing that they would then fall back, laughing and calling after her, unwilling to stray into a rival gang's area.

As so often happened to her in the evening, she felt weary and ineffectual as she unlocked the door to her home.

When she was tired the magnitude of the poverty all around seemed beyond anything that it was humanly possible to solve. However hard she worked she could do no more than temporarily scratch the surface for the few people she managed to reach. She had arrived in Rio feeling certain that she would be able to make a difference, but at moments like this she realised she had been ridiculously naive. Every day she met people who, like her, had started out believing they could make a big difference but had long since realised they couldn't. The negativity would sometimes drain her energy, making her feel helpless.

She threw her rucksack onto the mattress and collapsed, legs splayed, beside it. She felt consumed with frustration. She believed she was now getting to understand what NGO life was really like. If her experience was typical, then it was no wonder that nothing ever seemed to change for the very poor, despite the fact that NGOs had been around for decades. She knew that she would not be popular with her workmates if she spoke up, but she had to believe there was a better way to tackle poverty than what was currently taking place.

She told herself to snap out of it. She had put herself forward for this and so she had to stick with the programme and play ball, at least for the year. She stood up and lit the single lamp before setting the kettle to boil. A cockroach scurried across the floor but she barely noticed it. Her perception of what was normal had already changed beyond recognition. When she finally got to take her first sip of coffee she immediately felt better. There was nothing like local Brazilian coffee to be had anywhere in the fancy coffee shops she was used to frequenting in New York.

She had sat back down on the bed and had drifted into a daydream when she was startled back to the present by a knock as loud as a gunshot at the door. Occasionally kids would knock and then run like hell, but this sounded different. When it was mischievous kids they would barely tap the door before another little body dragged their arm away and there would be the sound of running feet and barely suppressed giggles. There was none of that cheeky adrenaline in this knock. It was confident and deliberate. Whoever was outside was not going to run away. Julia, along with all the other volunteers, had been warned not to answer her door if she was on her own after dark, so she didn't move, sitting on the bed as if frozen, hoping whoever it was would just go away.

"Julia," the voice said. "Is Gabriel. Please we can talk?"

"Gabriel," she called back, "what are you doing here? How did you know where I live? I cannot open the door. Come to the office tomorrow."

"Please. I speak to you now. Open the door, please."

"Are you alone?"

"Yes, yes."

Her thumping heart screamed that she was being stupid and taking too big a risk, but another part of it felt an urge to be kind to the man who had been given such a hard time by Maria a few hours before. She didn't want him to think that she was judging him too. But what if Maria was right and he was just another drug dealer? She took so long to make up her mind and get off the bed that he knocked again, a little more aggressively. Taking a deep breath, she walked across the room and unhooked the bolt, opening the door a crack.

Whatever swagger Gabriel had managed to put on when accosting Maria in the street had drained away. His shoulders were sagging and he was a little out of breath from climbing the hill and banging on the door. He looked even less like her idea of a drug dealer than he had in the daylight. Instinctively realising that he did not represent a threat, Julia felt anger at this encroachment on her home territory replacing her fear. This was not supposed to happen.

"What do you want?" she demanded.

"I'm very sorry for coming but I need to speak. You are lawyer, yes?"

"I think you already know that."

"And you think I am a drug dealer?"

"Actually I don't, no, but everyone else seems to. They tell me you made a lot of money, that you built a house and paid for a big wedding. How did you do that if it wasn't drugs?"

"I was paid by a doctor who stole something from me," he said. "I told Miss Morales."

"She told you she hadn't been able to find any evidence to back that story up," she said.

"I no drug dealer," he wailed, the passion in his voice taking her by surprise. "Never sell one single drug in all my life."

"OK, OK." She held her hand up to quieten him, glancing nervously down the street behind and hoping he wasn't attracting any attention from others who might sense the possibility of some late-night entertainment. The last thing she wanted was to let any more people know that a young foreign woman lived alone behind the blue door. "I told you, Gabriel

– I don't believe you are a drug dealer. I don't actually care how you made your money. That is your own business as far as I'm concerned. All I want to know is why you are knocking on my door this late at night."

"OK," he said, taking a deep breath as if preparing himself to tell his story all over again, already knowing that she wouldn't believe him any more than anyone else. "I don't have any job any more because I need to look after my wife and I'm tired. I am telling the truth about how I make money for a wedding. I do drug trial, with my wife. Medical trial and get a lot of money for it. It make me feel bad. My wife much worse. She is poisoned."

"What kind of trial?" she asked, her interest piqued despite herself. Although Maria had told her that she believed the story was a fabrication, something about the way he spoke made Julia think that Gabriel believed what he was saying.

"I no suppose to talk about it. I sign a paper. Trial is to do with my heart, I think."

"You think? You undertook a trial without being sure what it was about?"

"They give a lot of money and they were doctors, so I believe they wouldn't do anything bad. They showed us papers but we not able to read. But now I think my wife may be dying and it is my fault."

"How much money did you get?"

"They give five thousand US dollars each."

"Five thousand?" She was shocked and wondered if this wildly unlikely amount proved that he was lying. "How many of you were there?"

"Just me and my wife, Isabella. She was so beautiful that day, you would not believe..." For a second he seemed to literally swell with pride in front of her. "I've met others since who did the same thing. Many others, but most not paid so much. For us they must have done something extra, but we didn't understand because we not read the papers they gave us to sign."

"You're joking, right? Five thousand dollars each?"

Gabriel shook his head. He was not smiling. His eyes were fixed on the floor and it was obvious he was deeply depressed. "Now I no feel good," he said again. "And Isabella, she is much sicker."

"How long ago did this thing happen?" Julia asked.

He shrugged. 'About five years. Maybe six.'

"And she has been ill all this time?"

"It gets worse every day."

"You need to get her to see a doctor," she said, relieved at being able to think of a bit of useful advice for him, "not a damn lawyer."

She wondered if she should invite him in since he said he wasn't feeling well, before anyone else saw him standing on the doorstep, but that seemed like too big a risk.

"I took her to see a doctor but he say go to company that did test."

"And?"

"They gone."

"So what do you think I can do?"

"I need to find company. They need to tell me how to save my wife."

"Hasn't Maria already tried to do that for you?"

"Miss Morales thinks I am drug dealer. She thinks I lie. She does not try hard to find the people who did this."

"What's wrong with you exactly? When you say you feel bad, what do you mean?"

"Cannot explain. I change. Cannot explain. I get tired, like an old man."

"Listen, I'm sorry, but you should not be here – you have to leave."

Gabriel looked as if he was going to ask one more time and then all the air seemed to leave his body and he slumped against the door frame. Julia caught him before he fell to the floor and helped him inside, sitting him down on the chair, surprised by how light he was, little more than skin and bone. Only once she stood back to look at him did she realise what had happened. He had managed to get inside her house. She ran to the door and slammed it shut, suddenly fearful that others might take the opportunity to follow, then realised she had shut herself inside with a man she knew nothing about. She stood with her back to the door for a few moments, frozen with indecision, staring at him as he fought for breath, his eyes closed. Finally a little of his strength returned and he pulled himself into a more upright position. If he was acting, then he was very good at it.

"Sorry," he said. "I am so tired from looking after Isabella. She needs my help all the time."

"Would you like a coffee?" she asked.

He nodded and she topped up her cup before handing it to him. She sat on the edge of the bed and watched as he cradled it in both hands, bringing it up to his lips and taking a sip.

In the light of the lamp she could see how handsome he would be if it were not for the dark circles under his eyes and the shadows on his cheeks where the flesh seemed to have caved in. His nose was straight and fine looking and the lashes on his sunken brown eyes were as thick as a young girl's.

"I sorry," he said again after a few moments. "It is not your problem. Not your business to help us."

His words stung her conscience. "I want to help," she protested, "that's the whole point of me being here. I'm just not sure what I can do."

He shrugged as if he had nothing more to suggest.

"Would you like me to bring a doctor to see you and your wife? Someone more sympathetic than whomever you saw before."

He nodded. "Isabella stays in bed nearly all day now," he said.

"Where do you live?" she asked, giving him a piece of paper and pen. He drew a small map, showing that he was just in the next street. "OK," she said, "I will try to bring someone tomorrow."

Apparently satisfied, Gabriel put the cup down carefully on the table and heaved himself back onto his feet. Lacking the energy to say anything more he took Julia's hand and raised it to his lips as carefully as the coffee cup. She was surprised by the strength of the shiver that rippled through her body. As he shuffled towards the door his legs gave way beneath him once more and he lurched against the frame, only just saving himself from falling all the way to his knees. Julia grabbed him under the arms to support him.

"You'd better lie down," she said, gesturing towards the bed, no longer feeling remotely threatened by this shadow of a man.

"No"– he shook his head, taking a deep breath and pulling himself back up to his full height, holding his head up proudly – "I need to get back to Isabella. She will be worried."

"I'll help you."

It was only once she was outside the house in the dark, with Gabriel leaning heavily on her arm, that she realised she was being ridiculously rash going with a man she knew nothing about to his house, not even stopping to lock her own door behind her. Suppose he was lying to her and there were other men waiting? She told herself to stop being paranoid. She had volunteered to go with him, it hadn't been his idea, and he was obviously far too weak to overpower her in any way. Still, her heart was thumping fiercely as they made their way through the alleys and she was aware of many eyes watching their slow progress from the shadows. She was conscious that should anyone step forward to threaten them, Gabriel would not be strong enough to run or fight and she would have to defend them both.

They eventually reached Gabriel's family home and he led her up some concrete stairs to the first floor, pausing for breath on each step.

"My family live below with my mama," he explained. "I build this floor for my wife and me when we marry." She could hear in his voice how proud he was of his achievements, both the building of his home and the winning of his wife.

Inside the house, which was really just one room, a bare light bulb cast a white glare over the surprisingly clean and simple open space. The two of them obviously worked hard to look after their few belongings. The first thing that caught Julia's eye was an ornately framed wedding photo of the couple standing on the table, and she was shocked by how young, beautiful and vibrant they both looked. Their joyful smiles and unlined faces were a sharp contrast to the gaunt expression on Gabriel's face now. Had he really aged this much in just five years?

It was a few seconds before she realised that what she had taken for a pile of old clothes in the corner was actually the sleeping form of Isabella. Their noisy arrival into the room made her stir and she uncurled slowly, blinking as she tried to work out who Gabriel had brought home with him.

Gabriel explained to her in Portuguese and then introduced them. Julia shook Isabella's tiny outstretched hand and for a moment there was a flash of the same beauty she had seen in the photograph as the young bride smiled back. Isabella struggled to stand up and act like a hostess in her own home but Julia put out her hand to stop her.

"Please," she said, "don't get up. It's lovely to meet you both." She turned back to Gabriel. "I will find a doctor and bring them here, I promise."

"Thank you," he said and both of them watched as she made her way out and hurried back through the night to the familiar surroundings and relative safety of her own shack, once there bolting the door firmly behind her.

The incident had left her feeling uneasy on several levels. She had come to think of her home as her sanctuary from the dangers outside, but now she realised how easily the troubles of the outside world could infiltrate it. She wasn't sure she was ever going to be able to relax enough to sleep soundly there again, and the image of the exhausted-looking young couple kept coming back into her mind, along with the story Gabriel had told her. Was it really possible that international drug companies swooped into poor neighbourhoods, carried out dangerous drug trials and then simply disappeared, taking no responsibility for any damage they might have caused?

She couldn't believe that ethically-run corporations would be able to behave that way for long before someone exposed them, but the doubts would not leave her alone as she lay on her bed turning over in her mind all the things that could possibly go wrong with trials for untested drugs, from fatalities to disfigurement to ailments that did not show themselves until much later in the victims' lives. It felt like she should be doing something about it, but in her overtired, stressed state she couldn't think clearly what that something should be. Tears of frustration ran unchecked down her hot cheeks, dampening the pillow.

Chapter Seven

Ever since announcing his retirement, Geoff had been careful not to interfere with the day-to-day business of Madison and Partners unless one of the partners came to him with a specific question. He made it clear that his door at Oakdale was always open and he would always pick up the phone to anyone who wanted to take advantage of his experience. He was only half disappointed by how quickly the number of calls and visits started to dwindle. The other half of him felt pride that he had trained and empowered his partners and juniors so thoroughly and so effectively that they were able to take over the running of the company in an apparently seamless transition. He deliberately didn't ask Daniel Steinman any questions about progress on the latest Yokadus patent, not wanting to put the man under any more pressure than Geoff assumed Larry was already putting him under.

There had been a few rather awkward lunches with Larry as the two men attempted to maintain their lifelong friendship without mentioning the elephant in the room. It was obvious that Larry was totally obsessed with the developments of the new procedure and found it very hard to avoid talking about them. The more jocular Larry became, the more withdrawn and quiet Geoff grew, and the intervals between their meetings had become longer each time. It was almost as if an age gap had opened up between them as Geoff adapted to the third age of his life while Larry grew ever more youthful and energetic. It seemed likely to both of them that the damage done to their personal relationship was going to prove irreparable.

So Geoff learned at the same time as the rest of the world – or at least the part of the world that read the same academic journals and newspapers as him – that the patent had been approved and the FDA had approved clinical trials of Yokadus's revolutionary new process. At last, as he saw the details of the announcement published in black and white, he felt able to talk to Carole openly about why he had decided to retire early. He found her sitting on the terrace in the morning sun with a pot of coffee, reading a book.

"Would you read this?" he said, passing her the full-length article on the subject, which he had found in the *Harvard International Law Journal*. "I think it will interest you."

Carole was surprised by the request because Geoff knew that she took little interest in legal issues, but she put her book aside and took the magazine from him. As she started reading, Geoff strolled down the garden to the beach to give her some time to take in what he was revealing to her. It was only when she was about halfway through the article that she realised what he was telling her. She looked up for a moment and saw him standing beside the water, staring out to sea, apparently lost in his own thoughts, and was surprised by how small he looked. She read on to the end of the article and then poured herself a fresh coffee and went back to the beginning and read through the whole thing again. By the time her husband came back across the lawn she had put the magazine down and was staring at the trees, lost in thought. Geoff sat down beside her, still not saying anything.

"Is this what you and Larry fell out about?" she asked eventually.

"I'm not sure I would say we exactly 'fell out'," he replied.

"Is it the reason you retired early?"

"Yes."

She picked up the article and stared at it again, as if trying to work out what she was thinking before saying anything further.

"So," she said finally, "they have discovered a way that people can buy more time for themselves – a medical procedure?"

"That's correct. It is also a way that people can sell time. If you are poor and you need money, and you don't mind shortening your lifespan, Yokadus claim they have developed a way to extract time from your metabolism." He traced a circle around his heart with his index finger. "It then becomes a product that can be stored and sold on the market. At the moment they cannot sell it legally in this country, or any other First World countries, but if they can get approval, they will be the only ones with the patent to go to market. It will be the biggest monopoly since the Silicon Valley giants first rose up.

"It will create a whole new market, just like oil did, and coal before that, and data—"

He was about to list more discoveries that had led to large-scale changes in the distribution of wealth, but Carole held up her hand to stop him. She needed more time to think through what he was telling her.

"So those who can afford to buy this commodity will be able to live longer and more productive lives?"

"Correct."

"And those who need the money can accept payment in exchange for shortening their lives – lives that would be of a low quality if they had to be endured in poverty?"

"Correct."

"So it would transfer a great deal of wealth from those who are financially rich but time poor to those who are trapped in the opposite situation?"

"That is certainly how Yokadus – and Larry – see it."

"But you disagree?"

"I have severe reservations about the ethics of such an operation. I can see the logic of it, but … Time is the only thing that people with money have not so far been able to buy. They have been able to extend their lifespans with better healthcare and better foods and so on, but they have not been able to actually buy time in a direct transaction with someone else. If they are allowed to do that, then the social divide between rich and poor will become a hundred times wider than it is at the moment. The richest people will be able to live virtually for ever, as long as the poor agree to die earlier than nature intended. If you take that to its logical conclusion, you will eventually find you have eradicated the poor, not poverty."

"A sort of process of unnatural selection?"

"Precisely."

"So Yokadus are claiming they have done the research with animals and have now been cleared to work on human guinea pigs, is that right?"

"That is what they're saying. By releasing the information, however, they have changed everything. Can you imagine how huge the demand will be among those who can afford it? These are people who will not be keen to wait for things to go through the long, slow approval processes. They will be wanting the product now. There could be enormous benefits too, I can't deny that. Imagine if a great doctor or a great scientist could live for an extra twenty or thirty productive years. Imagine what they could achieve."

"But of course we both know that not all rich people are that useful," Carole said ruefully. "There are a lot of people who would just want to live longer to consume more and enjoy themselves more, without adding any value to the rest of the world. I could name quite a few myself."

"Exactly. That's also true. It is certainly not a black and white situation. What is certain is that it will create a whole new economy, a huge shift in the wealth from those who have it already to those who don't and who have nothing else to sell. A parent in the developing world, for instance, could sell enough time to afford to put their children through university or to build them a family home when now they're living on the street. The potential is enormous. If someone raises money by selling time, starts a business and becomes rich, they will be able to buy back the time later on. All young people believe they are going to be rich one day, so that will lure a lot of them into selling far more than they should, believing that they will be able to put things right later. Of course, most won't be able to do that but will already have done the damage to their bodies."

"They will have sold their souls to the devil..."

"In a manner of speaking, yes."

As always, like any great lawyer, Geoff was anxious to examine both sides of the case before rushing to any premature judgements. He wanted Carole to search her own conscience and come to her own conclusions as to whether she agreed with his decision to have nothing to do with Larry's plans.

"The rich will be able to buy the lives of the poor to enjoy for themselves." Carole was still trying to get her head round the concept. "I understand the logic of that. But what if there are not enough people willing to sell?"

"Then I guess the price would continue to rise until they could no longer resist the temptation. Or people would start finding other ways to harvest the time – like mugging people for their kidneys. They might even start breeding children specifically to harvest their time."

"Stealing people's natural lifespans from them? That's amazing, but appalling."

"That was exactly my dilemma."

It felt like a huge weight had been lifted from his shoulders now that he could share the burden he had been carrying for so long with the person whose judgement in such matters he trusted the most.

"But Madison and Partners have been continuing to work on the patent without you?"

"They have. I left it up to the consciences of the individuals concerned."

Carole stood up and put her arms around him. "You poor old thing. This has really taken its toll on you, hasn't it?"

Geoff didn't reply, simply holding onto her tightly as he stared down the garden towards the sea.

Chapter Eight

It was actually several days before Julia was able to find a doctor who was willing to come out to the favelas with her. There were many medical specialists attached to PSG whom she approached first, but they were all overworked, and when she told them the story of Gabriel and Isabella they were sceptical and half-hearted in their responses. None of them wanted to take the time to go out into the favelas and research the problem. It seemed to her that they had heard stories like this before and they had already set their minds against giving them credence. They avoided her eye when she asked them if that was the case, as if they had something to hide, as if they were implicated in some way. Was she imagining it? Was Maria right and Gabriel had managed to get inside her brain and make her believe in his imagined conspiracy plot?

Julia decided there was no point taking up a doctor's expensive time if they already had the wrong attitude. The last thing she wanted was to get the young couple's hopes up and then let them down with inaction further down the line. They had suffered enough of that already. She wanted to find someone with an open mind who would listen to what Gabriel had to say without making judgements.

In the end she decided that she was going to have to use her own initiative and go beyond the PSG network. She made appointments with several private doctors in the city, visiting all of them without telling Maria or the other workers what she was doing. She paid for their consulting time out of her own money.

Having an American lawyer willing to foot the bill meant that all the private doctors she went to see were happy to take on the job, but there was something about each of them that didn't feel quite right to her. These doctors looked her in the eye but there was something brazen about the way they faced her down. They were altogether too prosperous looking, their consulting rooms too shiny and clean, too much like the rooms Gabriel and Isabella had described to her. If their story was true, it was possible that any one of these people she was now sitting in front of was the doctor who actually performed the procedure on them.

She couldn't imagine that any of them would be willing to fight for a couple like Gabriel and Isabella against a multinational pharmaceutical company, should things ever come to that. They might even try to discredit the story for their own reasons.

On the third day of looking, however, while walking back to the bus in the late afternoon, she noticed a sign pointing down a small back street to a free clinic. Out of curiosity she followed the sign through the canyon of glass buildings until she came to what looked like a series of garages with people queuing outside. She wandered closer, trying to look inconspicuous. Most of the people in the queue were too old or too ill to even look up as she passed, many of them sitting with their backs against the wall, their eyes closed, their energies drained.

"Can I help you?" asked a slim young woman in a white coat and round glasses that made her eyes look enormous.

"I'm looking for a doctor."

"Are you ill?"

"It's for a friend, well, two friends, a young couple who are very ill."

"Too ill to come here and join the queue?"

"Are you Australian?" Julia asked, trying to place the accent.

"English. My name is Amy. I'm one of the doctors here."

Julia held out her hand and Amy shook it, looking a little puzzled.

"Yes," Julia said, "I think they may be too ill. Her, at least. He could get here but he's her full-time carer. They have a strange story about being hired to do some sort of test for a pharmaceutical company, which they now believe has made them ill."

"Really?" Julia could see she had the young doctor's attention. "Are they willing to talk about it?"

"Yes, I think so. Well, he is anyway."

"They've not been threatened into silence?"

"No. Why would you say that?"

"Because most of these people are too frightened to say a word." Amy gestured at the crowd. "But one or two of them have suggested something similar to what you are describing."

Julia turned to look more closely at the queue of patients waiting for medical attention and realised that they had very much the same look in their eyes that she had seen in Gabriel's and Isabella's eyes.

"Would you have time to come and see them?"

"I'll make time," Amy said. "How about this evening?"

"That would be great. I'm happy to pay you."

"Don't worry about that. Maybe you can buy me a beer afterwards."

"You bet."

Amy was obviously more accustomed to walking around the backstreets in the shadows of the evening than Julia. She made a point of always staring ahead and keeping up a brisk pace, giving no indication that she had heard the catcalls or shouts of abuse from the doorways and corners. Gabriel and Isabella were downstairs eating with the rest of the family when they knocked on the door. Julia introduced them and Amy examined both of them despite the number of people sitting around watching in awed silence. Julia was impressed by how gentle and professional Amy was as she talked to them and laid her hands and stethoscope on their hearts.

"I'm going to leave you with some painkillers," she said once she was satisfied there was nothing urgent to be dealt with. "And if you are able to get to my clinic, I will be able to keep you supplied regularly. Julia will tell you where it is."

Everyone thanked her profusely and she and Julia made their way back down to the first street they could find a bar where two foreign women on their own would not stick out like sore thumbs.

"So what is wrong with them?" Julia asked, once she had ordered the beers.

"I've no idea," Amy admitted, "but their symptoms are very similar to the ones I see at the clinic all day long. "It is extremely likely that whatever it is was caused by whatever tests they undertook, but until someone finds out what those tests were, there is no way of knowing how to treat the symptoms. The painkillers will help a lot with the aching joints, and that should lessen the feelings of tiredness a bit, but it can hardly be called a cure."

"He said they were paid five thousand dollars each," Julia said.

Amy let out a low whistle. "That is a lot," she said, "but that may explain why they are so ill. It seems that those who were paid the most have become sickest. It is as if the people doing the testing offered money as compensation, a small amount to make them a little sick, a large amount to make them more sick—"

"Or make them sick faster."

"Exactly. It may be that the people who were just paid a few hundred dollars haven't even noticed the symptoms because they have come on so slowly."

"Isabella is much sicker than Gabriel, though, and they were paid the same amount."

"I guess her resistance was lower. Maybe he was just stronger than her. If you donate a kidney to someone and your other kidney is fine, then you will feel no ill effects. But if your remaining kidney is not healthy, you will start to feel the side effects of the operation very quickly."

"So what are these people doing to their guinea pigs?"

"I can't quite work it out and the only theory I've managed to come up with is so far-fetched I would be embarrassed to say it out loud to anyone."

"Would another beer loosen your tongue?"

"It might," the doctor said laughing, "but you will think I'm mad when I tell you."

"Try me."

Amy took a deep breath. "I think it may be this thing that has been in the news recently. I think they may be extracting time from people, shortening their lifespans and selling it as a product to those who can afford it. I think they aren't very skilled at it yet and that's why they're sometimes taking too much time and making some people age much too fast. Alternatively, they may be very skilled indeed and know exactly what they are doing but don't care about the people who they are basically killing."

Julia's jaw dropped and she said nothing as she tried to take in the ramifications of what she was hearing.

"I told you you'd think I was mad."

"But they would have to ask permission, surely, before performing a procedure like that?"

"I dare say they got them all to sign contracts agreeing to everything, ignoring the fact that half of them can't read and the ones who can wouldn't bother to study the small print if it meant they had to wait for their payment. None of us read the small print in contracts, right? That's why lawyers put it there, to get us to agree to things without realising it."

"I'm a lawyer."

"Oh, well then you know that better than anyone. No offence."

"None taken because I'm afraid I know you are right."

"So I still get my second beer?"

"Sure."

Julia called for two more beers.

* * * * *

Carole had developed a habit of calling Julia every Sunday evening. She would have liked to talk to her daughter every day, but she knew that was too invasive. If Julia wanted to talk to her, she could always call, but she never wanted to be the kind of mom who was constantly bothering her adult children. Julia enjoyed the calls, even though they sometimes left her feeling a little homesick, and she actually wouldn't have minded receiving more. They gave her something to look forward to on the evenings she was in the shack on her own. She would speak to her dad when he was around and her mum passed him the phone. From the things they didn't say as much as the things they did say, it seemed to Julia that retirement was presenting challenges for both of them.

Carole never said, but she was increasingly anxious to get Julia back to the US, even though with each passing month she became more used to the idea of her being several thousand miles away. Julia was careful always to talk up the good things about Rio, letting her mother know that she was enjoying the experience and not mentioning the more challenging aspects, like the moments she felt totally alone and deeply inadequate in the face of the job that needed done. The feelings of fulfilment, by and large, did outweigh the hardships and the frustrations, but only some of the time.

Julia loved it when Geoff came on the line during those calls, even though he never had much to say. Her admiration for her father had been unwavering since she was a little girl. Although she wouldn't have understood it as a child, she knew now that it was his moral courage that she admired the most, which made the world feel like a safe place when he was around. She had simply never met anyone else to match him, and even as a rebellious teenager she had constantly measured her own behaviour against how she knew he would act in any given situation. Some friends, particularly when emboldened by alcohol, had suggested in the past that one of the reasons she was still single was that she had never met anyone who could match up to her father. As the years ticked by she was beginning to think they might have a point.

Gabriel's story had been going round and round in her head ever since the night he came knocking on her door and she wondered how her father would have reacted if it had been him who Gabriel had confided in. Was Gabriel a credible witness? So much of the story that he told didn't make sense. If he had taken part in a medical drug trial as he claimed, why didn't he have access to his medical records and other data? But by even asking herself that question, was she showing how far removed she was as a privileged Manhattan lawyer from understanding what life was like for someone at the bottom of the social pile in a place like Rio?

After the evening in the bar with Amy, Julia had given a lot of thought to the idea of companies extracting time from volunteers and selling it. Initially she had been half inclined to put it down to late-night bar talk, a product of too many beers, but the more she thought about it the more it seemed to explain the situation that Gabriel and Isabella now found themselves in.

"Hi, J," Geoff said when Carole handed him the phone that Sunday evening. "How's things in Rio? Getting anywhere with your plans to save the world?"

"Well, you know how it is, Dad," she laughed, happy to hear his voice. "Some things change mighty slowly. One step forwards, two steps backwards. Listen, Dad, I wanted to run something past you. What do you know about drug trials?"

"What do you mean, J?"

"You know, when drug companies use volunteers to test drugs."

"What do you want to know?"

"Well, it's just that there are some people down here who claim they agreed to do some tests a few years back and now they regret it. They say they don't feel right. They certainly don't look right, not for their age. Some of them are in a really bad way. But when they tried to contact the relevant drug company, the one they claim did the tests, it was gone. Totally vanished."

"Do you believe their stories?"

"Some of it seems far-fetched, but they seem consistent."

"Far-fetched how?"

"They claim they were paid five thousand dollars just for one test. I know that doesn't sound like much, but down here it can build you a house."

"Say that again."

"Down here that can build you a house."

"Did you just say five thousand dollars?"

"Yes, that's what they got paid."

"No, J. That can't be true. Five hundred maybe. Not five thousand, I can assure you."

"I'm telling you, Dad. It's five thousand. The guy I've been talking to paid for his wedding from this. I've seen it with my own eyes."

"What is the test?"

"They aren't sure. They think it is something to do with the heart. It was in that area anyway."

"Sounds damn risky. Did they sign their lives away? Are there any symptoms?"

"I've called in this English doctor who says she has seen any number of cases just like theirs and she's pretty convinced they're telling the truth. She can't tell what's wrong with them, just that they seem old and tired before their time. Exhausted. Aching joints, difficulty sleeping, bladder trouble. All sorts of things. It just seems strange to me that a pharmaceutical company would pay out large sums of money and then vanish into thin air when people come back with complaints and questions. This doctor has some theories of her own, but they are pretty wacky."

"What sort of theories?"

"That they are extracting time – like they are talking about in the news – but they're taking it from people who aren't being informed and then selling it at inflated prices. The reason they're paying so much is because they're still experimenting and learning. In some cases they are taking too much and some of the volunteers are ageing much too fast. There is one girl in particular who I've met, and she is like a dying old woman and she's only in her early thirties. She's one of the ones who got paid five thousand dollars."

Geoff fell silent for a few seconds and when he started speaking again he sounded like a professional lawyer talking to a client rather than a father talking to his daughter. "There have been some articles published in the legal and medical journals," he said. "You wouldn't have seen them down there. I'll send them to you. They will give you a better idea about how this time-trading thing works. The stuff in the mainstream media is too sensationalist. The media are looking for controversy not scientific facts."

"So this time-trading is a real thing?"

"Well, it's not supposed to be, not yet. They're trying to make it legal. You'll understand when you see the articles. I don't know too much about drug-trialling laws in South America – I will have to do some research."

"Dad, don't go to too much trouble. I may not even have the chance to read them."

"Listen, what else have I got to do?" He laughed, and she could hear her mother commenting in the background. "OK, I won't, but it should be relatively easy to research. Wouldn't take long. What do your friends at PSG have to say about this?"

"They don't believe any of it, but they haven't seen or heard as much as I have. They have enough on their plates just dealing with people's ordinary day-to-day problems. They haven't got time to look into conspiracy theories which might prove to be no more than that. The medical professionals I've talked to, however, seem to be extremely furtive about the whole thing. Apart from this English girl."

"J, if this is outside the remit of PSG, don't go there. It could be anything and it could be dangerous, especially if people are making big money. They won't want someone like you poking around. I know you believe you are invincible, but you are still a girl on her own in a foreign city that has a high murder rate."

"I'm a grown woman now, Dad, not a girl."

"You'll always be my girl, J. Just humour an old man and be a little careful."

"I know, Dad. Don't worry, I won't do anything stupid."

Geoff didn't email the material to Julia for several days because he wanted to think through the implications of what she had told him. He talked about it with Carole who was predictably furious at the idea of a big rich pharmaceutical company messing with the lives of poor young people without their permission, and paying them off with a few thousand dollars.

"Could it be anything to do with Yokadus?" Carole asked, the tone of her voice suggesting that she thought it was.

"That's too easy a conclusion to jump to," Geoff said. "There are a lot of big, ruthless companies out there who would be more than capable of doing something like this. If Yokadus is going down this path, you can be sure their rivals aren't far behind."

"Is it possible that if it was Yokadus, Larry would know nothing about it?"

Geoff didn't answer for a while. It was a question he had been asking himself. "You know Larry," he said eventually with a resigned shrug.

"If it is Yokadus," Carole said slowly, as if still thinking it through as she talked, "and if Larry signed off on it, he should be prosecuted. The fact that he's your oldest friend can't come into it."

"But it's not actually my responsibility to expose him, is it?" Geoff sounded doubtful.

"It might be if you are the only person who has made the connection. If you wait until the whole business has been legalised, it will be much harder to stop. This could be an opportunity to prevent things going any further, or at least to slow them down."

Julia was not surprised when her father called her again a few days later to ask for more information about the drug trials. One of the best things about him was that he was always interested in everything that came to his attention. It had been great when she and her brothers were small. Whatever they might be chattering about over the breakfast or dinner table, he would have follow-up questions for them. He showed them that he was interested in everything they did and everything they said, whether it was grumbling about someone at school being nasty to them, boasting about a sporting achievement or voicing a worry about homework. He always wanted to know more. Often he would come back from work with a book or a magazine that answered whatever questions they had been asking.

He called her at a time when he was pretty sure she would be home alone.

"I just emailed you that stuff. Did you talk to these people again?"

"No, I didn't see them. I've been busy. There's so much to do down here, Dad, so many people needing help."

"I know, I know." Geoff felt a twinge of regret at the relative idleness which had taken over his life since he stopped going to the office. Whenever he said anything to Carole about how useless he was feeling she would point out that he still did far more than most of their contemporaries – sitting on the boards of charities – but it didn't make him feel any better. "Can you get me more information? What exactly did the tests involve? Where did they take place? Exactly what symptoms are the people displaying?"

"I'll do my best, Dad," Julia said laughing, "but I can't be sure that anything I'm being told by anyone is true."

"That's why it's good you trained as a lawyer," Geoff teased, "so you are able to root out the truth."

"Not everyone sees things the same way, though. One man's truth is another man's fantasy."

"That's what makes the law so damn interesting as a profession."

"OK, Dad." She laughed again. "I get the message. I'll try to get you some answers. Leave it with me."

Spurred on by the phone call, Julia opened up her father's email and started to read about time-trading and the clinical trials. The medical side of it was new territory for her but because of her legal training she was able to follow what was being said, and found herself being drawn into a new world, only pausing to refresh her coffee as the hours ticked by and the night finally grew silent outside.

She found it difficult to reconcile the things that Gabriel had told her with what she was reading. The types of trials described in the literature, either as observational studies or interventional studies, required continued contact with the subject after the trials themselves. Alternative classifications such as prevention, screening, diagnostic or treatment trials required similar amounts of ongoing contact. Even if you disagreed with the concept of time-trading, you had to admit that what was claimed looked ethical and above board.

It seemed that clinical trials were commonly classified into four phases and each phase of the drug-approval process was treated as a separate clinical trial. As a result of all these stages, the process was inevitably slow. An essential component of initiating a clinical trial was always to recruit study subjects following procedures using a signed document called "informed consent". Informed consent was a legally defined process whereby a person was required to be told about the key facts involved in a clinical trial before deciding whether or not to participate. None of this seemed to be the case with the experience Gabriel and Isabella had described to her, but it was possible she needed to ask more in-depth questions and that the language barrier might have meant she'd misunderstood some of what they were trying to tell her.

Eventually she reached the end of the reading material and turned off the screen. She wished she had someone there she could talk to about it. She tried to think of someone at PSG other than Maria who might be able to shed some light on the subject, but she couldn't think of anyone. She thought about calling Beatriz, but when she rehearsed in her head what she would say it all sounded ludicrous. It would be great to discuss it, but she knew she would be told to walk away. "It's not within our scope" they would tell her, using words like "procedures", "guidelines", "protocols" or whatever they chose to call them. There always seemed to be a word to restrict the activities of individuals working for NGOs and other charitable organisations and to discourage them from following up on anything new they might come across. She supposed that was inevitable, otherwise there would be no end to the things they would find themselves being asked to do. The problems in communities like the favelas were so great and so multiple, each organisation had to have its own niche and speciality to achieve any visible results.

She was woken by a firm knocking on her door. She could see surprisingly bright spots of light in the various holes in the roof, which suggested it was later than she usually woke up. Glancing at her phone she saw it was ten o'clock, an unheard of lie-in for her. The heat had already built up in the room and she was drenched in sweat as she walked to the door. Fanning herself with her T-shirt, she tried to squint through a crack.

"Who is it?"

"Is Gabriel."

She was surprised by how pleased she was to hear his voice and she unlocked the door to let him in. It no longer seemed inappropriate that he was coming into her house. It felt more like a visit from a friend. He looked much stronger than when she last saw him, but he still sank into the chair with a grateful sigh, as if anxious to rest his joints after the short walk from his house.

"Have the painkillers Dr Amy gave you helped?"

"Yes, I think so. She was kind to come and see us. Thank you for bringing her."

Julia brewed them both cups of coffee while he watched her and rested. Julia found herself asking questions in the same way as she might a client back in Manhattan.

"When did you first hear of these trials?"

"There was an advertisement in a newspaper, which had an address to go to."

"Do you still have the advertisement?"

He shook his head. "Someone showed it to me. I don't read."

"Had you heard of the trials before?"

"I had heard people talking about being paid for medical procedures, but never so much money. Most people would hear from a friend or a relative and would go to an address with someone else."

"Do you remember the address you went to?"

"No, but I could take you there. We went first for examination. Then we were given another address to go to for the trial. I could take you there too."

For the next hour or two Gabriel struggled to describe every detail of his trip into the city with Isabella and to tell Julia exactly what he remembered of the procedure itself, which was virtually nothing.

"So talk to me about the symptoms. How you started to feel ill."

"To start with we felt fine. No problems. We were so happy to have the money. We arranged the wedding and we built the extra floor on the house and made downstairs more comfortable for my mother and my grandmother and my brothers and sisters. All the family helped with the plumbing and the building. We bought a good air-conditioning unit. It was a happy time. Isabella was the most beautiful bride."

"I saw the wedding picture."

"Yes. But then we both started to feel tired all the time. My arms and my legs ached whenever I climbed the hill, but with Isabella it was much, much worse. She started to move as slow as my grandmother. Life was no fun anymore because I was always tired and always aching. I felt like an old man. Isabella often stayed in bed all day and her beauty started to disappear before my eyes. My thinking is different. I do not want to do the things I used to do before. Perhaps I'm just maturing, but most of the people I know who are my age are still acting like they are teenagers. Isabella is now like an invalid, like you saw. We spent all the money in the first year and now we have no way of earning any more, so we have to depend on our families for food and anything else we need. Everyone tries to help, but no one has anything to spare."

Even if she could find out who had done the procedure, Julia couldn't imagine how she would be able to make a case for damages from the company out of such vague descriptions and no medical tests to compare. She could just picture the judge's expression if she tried. After Gabriel had gone, she tried to remember everything he had told her and put it in an email to her father.

She was surprised the following Sunday evening when her father called again instead of her mother. For a second she panicked that something might be wrong at home, but then she realised it was just that Geoff had more questions for her. If she was being honest, she had put the matter to the back of her mind since sending the email, working at full tilt on things where she could make an immediate difference to people's daily lives. She had put the whole thing down to some kind of small-scale industrial or medical malpractice without significantly bad outcomes to warrant a full investigation. Her dad, on the other hand, seemed animated at the prospect of discussing the issue.

"Can you tell me more about your friend Gabriel's symptoms?"

"Not really," she admitted. "I put it all in the email. He just says he feels older."

"Older?"

"Yes. He said he doesn't feel like his friends. He says his wife now moves like his grandmother, which, having met her, I would say is a pretty good description. Six years ago she was this radiant young girl, now she's this bedridden old woman."

"OK," he said, after a surprisingly long pause. "Let me pass you to your mother."

She and her mother gossiped for a while before saying goodnight.

It was only three days later that Geoff called his daughter again and told her the whole story of why he had retired and why he and Larry McMahon had fallen out. He said that the things she had been telling him worried him.

"I think they are already stealing time from people who have no idea what they are agreeing to, people like your friends. But I don't think they really know what they're doing, so they're making mistakes. You and your doctor friend could be right that they are extracting far too much time from some people – like the girl you described."

"Isabella."

"Yes. It may be they took so much time, they have used up nearly everything that was allotted to her by nature. Or it may be that she had some underlying condition, which they didn't test for before doing the procedure, and that means she was never going to live that long anyway, and now they have dramatically hastened the process. If that is the case, and it can be proved, then all the people who were used as guinea pigs would be due considerable compensation. If there are a lot of them, then the bill could run into billions, which is why the companies – and doctors – involved are likely to deny everything and cover their tracks wherever possible. None of them are going to be happy that you are asking questions."

Julia was shocked, but at the same time excited to think there might actually be something she could do to help people like Gabriel and Isabella after all.

"This must have been such a huge burden for you and Mom to carry around," she said, "knowing that Larry might be behind it."

"I don't know for sure if he's behind this illegal trading," Geoff said, "but he is certainly behind the push to make it legal. It has been hard, and it is causing a big potential conflict of interest at the firm, but now I think it's time for us to share our concerns and do something more positive about it. I've been out of Madison and Partners for long enough now for that link to be truly severed. What is going on here is wrong and needs to be stopped, or at least slowed down."

"It's like it was meant to be," Julia said, "me coming to Rio and stumbling across Gabriel and my ties to you and the knowledge that you have. It's like some greater force has been weaving a web."

"Maybe," Geoff said laughing.

"How else could this have occurred without some sort of divine guidance?"

"There are some things for which even lawyers have to admit there is no explanation."

Julia knew he was teasing her, but it was an idea that she would come back to many times during the next few years, particularly during the low times when she needed some reason to keep on fighting.

"Don't speak to anyone about this," Geoff instructed, "until I get there."

"You're coming down to Rio?"

"Of course. Your mother could do with a break from my constant presence around the house."

Julia did not feel like informing her colleagues at PSG that her father was coming, which made her feel like she was lying to them about what she was doing, but Rio was a big enough place for them not to find out. And why should she feel she had to report a private visit from her father anyway? These were the reasons she gave herself, but the more she thought about the attitude of the doctors she had spoken to, the more she felt it would be wiser if they were not alerted to the fact that she and her father were on to them.

When she met him at the airport he was carrying only a leather briefcase and a small weekend bag. He was dressed more casually than he would have been had he been going to the office, but he was still as neat and smart as she remembered him always being. It was a strange moment for Julia, greeting him as an equal and a colleague rather than a father or a boss. For the first time she felt responsible for the outcome of something that she had initiated and which was now consuming family time and resources.

He seemed smaller and thinner than she remembered as he came towards her across the concourse, and there were more lines on his face than she remembered. She told herself that was ridiculous and he couldn't have changed that much in such a short time. It must be that she just hadn't looked that closely at him for a long time. Amidst all the trappings of the office, when dressed up in his power suits, he had always looked so powerful and in control; in a busy airport, wearing chinos and a polo shirt, he was just one more middle-aged travelling businessman. If he had lost weight it was probably because he no longer went to all those business lunches and dinners. If anyone had changed it was more likely to be her.

They embraced and she held onto him tightly, surprised by how emotional she felt. She hadn't realised quite how much of a strain living in the favela had been, always having to be alert, never being able to fully relax, never really totally comfortable, not having her father in the background to protect her. No wonder the people who lived there all their lives aged so quickly. Poverty was exhausting.

"I've rented a car," Geoff said. "Let's go look for it."

As they walked, they were already talking about their plans, both of them unable to hide their anger at the injustice of what they were discovering and their excitement at being on an adventure together.

"I need to leave PSG," Julia told him, "if I'm going to be spending all my time on this, but then I will have to find somewhere to live."

"You can stay at the hotel with me," Geoff said, "and stay on there after I've gone if necessary, but once we have all the facts we are going to have to go back to the US to go after these bastards."

"Do you think it is Yokadus?"

"Too early to say, but it's certainly possible, and if it is, then we have to go after them just as hard as we would any other company that's breaking the law and exploiting people on this scale."

"It could damage Madison and Partners. Yokadus could pull their business or even counter sue."

"Sometimes you have to do what you know is right, J, otherwise the bullies will always win."

"You mean Larry?"

He didn't say any more as they entered the car hire office.

"OK," Geoff said once they were driving out of the airport, "you know the routes around here. Let's go find your friend."

"Gabriel?"

"If that's his name."

"Don't you want to go to your hotel and maybe take a shower and rest up from the flight first?"

"I'm retired, J, not an invalid. Let's go."

They got as close to Gabriel's house as they could and parked, Geoff staying with the car while Julia went to find Gabriel and Isabella. They were both taking an afternoon nap, but felt well enough to get up and come with her to the car. Isabella leaned heavily on her husband's arm and needed to stop frequently to catch her breath. Julia helped her onto the seat in the back of the car and introduced them to her father.

"Do you think you can find the place where they did the initial examination?" she asked them.

"Sure," Isabella spoke for both of them. If anything she seemed even angrier than Gabriel about what had happened to them. She had expected to have started a family by now, but she no longer felt able to bear children or strong enough to look after them. She felt that someone had robbed her and her unborn children of their lives. That she didn't know who that person was made her even angrier. With her eyes blazing from the effort of getting up and walking to the car, it wasn't hard for Geoff and Julia to see just how beautiful she had been as a girl.

For the rest of the afternoon the four of them drove through the Rio traffic, taking many wrong turns and struggling to find places to park so they could get out and talk to people. They eventually found the travel agency, behind which the temporary consulting room had been set up. The room was empty now, but it was still possible to see traces of the equipment which had made it look like a professional doctor's room.

They thought they would come up against an elaborate cover-up when they started looking into who had hired the place, but it wasn't that hard. It seemed that whoever the people were they were not frightened of being traced. Perhaps it had not occurred to anyone working locally that they would ever be of interest to anyone. The travel agent had the name of the property management company that had handled the deal and the following day Geoff made contact with them. They happily gave up the name of a medical research company, Medical Laboratories Inc., who they said had been their client. When Geoff and Julia went to the head office of the medical research company, which was housed at an address in a nondescript street full of characterless offices and light industrial units, they were told that information on their clients was confidential.

"Can I see your senior legal officer?" Geoff asked, his manner making it clear that he was not leaving the premises until he had.

The man who came down to reception a few minutes later looked like he had just woken up from a siesta. At first he spouted the same line about confidentiality.

"Let me explain something," Geoff said after a few minutes of getting nowhere. "If you do not give up the client's name, it will be your company that will be sued for compensation by the victims. The bill that is likely to be lying in wait at the end of this investigation will be running into many millions. Can you afford to take on that sort of financial challenge?"

"Please take a seat," the legal officer replied, "while I talk to some people."

After only a few hurried phone calls to other members of his board, he returned with copies of emails which showed they had been employed by Yokadus. Their task, the emails informed them, was to identify as many likely donors as possible, referring them on to a variety of clinics and offering them a fee for their time. There was also an agreement that they would be paid a commission for each person they successfully recruited and the larger the amount of time each subject could be persuaded to part with, the higher those payments would be.

"That would explain the recruitment stage of this operation," Geoff said as they made their way back to the car with the papers safely tucked into his pocket. "Now let's find the bastards who actually did the stealing."

The glistening white clinic that Gabriel and Isabella remembered attending on the twenty-second floor of the glass tower downtown had also disappeared, the floor having been re-let to a fashion house from Milan specialising in expensive knitwear. In exchange for a few discreetly folded banknotes, the uniformed man on reception was happy to furnish Geoff with the telephone number of the management company and once again the trail led right back to Medical Laboratories. The receptionist also told them that he had seen many young people matching Gabriel and Isabella's description heading into the elevators to attend appointments.

"How many would you estimate?" Julia asked.

"Many, many."

"Dozens?"

"Oh, no" – the man laughed at her innocence – "many hundreds."

Geoff and Julia then spent several days at Dr Amy's street clinic, coaxing information out of the exhausted and frightened patients who were waiting for painkillers and other medical aid for symptoms that they couldn't understand or even describe clearly. At a casual glance they looked like geriatrics but once Geoff and Julia won their confidence and started them talking it was obvious they were all still young. Many of them seemed afraid to be seen talking to anyone who might be in a position of authority; as if they believed they might have committed a crime by asking for medical help, without knowing what the crime was. Those who were finally persuaded to give details told stories that were remarkably similar to Gabriel and Isabella's.

* * * * *

Within a week of arriving in Rio, Geoff was convinced that his suspicions were right. Larry's company had been paying people who were conducting experiments on human guinea pigs long before it was legal for them to do so, and long before the procedure had been proven safe. The result was all too plain to see in the ruined lives of people like Gabriel and Isabella. He was now convinced that whatever happened he had to find a way to stop time-trading becoming legal in the US, which meant stopping Larry. That was a daunting prospect because he, more than anyone in the world, knew just how formidable a foe Larry could be if he felt his ambitions were being thwarted.

If they were going to be taking legal action, the police in Rio and the regulatory authorities in the USA and Brazil were going to have to be informed, but the timings of such legal requirements were hazy and Geoff and Julia knew that they would be at a disadvantage dealing with people entrenched in a system they did not fully understand. They both needed to be safely back on US soil before they launched any sort of full-frontal attack against such an unknown, and potentially well-connected, enemy. There was no knowing who might have been paid off amongst the senior police officers and government officials in Rio, and it would not be hard for a couple of American visitors to disappear if they were known to be poking their noses too far into other people's business.

Once they were back in the US with their evidence they would be on more familiar territory, although both of them were aware that it was as easy for someone with as much money as Yokadus to hire an assassin in the US as anywhere else. Their removal would probably be set up as a fatal car crash rather than a total disappearance, but the final result would still be the same. Their best protection was to get the story into the media and ensure that the prosecution was launched quickly and irrevocably. Once that had happened, any "accident" that might befall them would immediately look suspect.

They just needed to demonstrate how the system in cities like Rio worked to start a credible prosecution. Geoff was convinced that if time was being harvested from the poor in one low-income country, it was highly likely that the same was going on in many others. If they could expose the system in Rio, then other people would start to come forward with stories from other places. To make their story more credible, however, they believed they needed to see the process in action with their own eyes, ideally with photographs as well. Simply coming forward with stories from frightened and inarticulate victims was unlikely to be enough. Apart from anything else, the witnesses would be too easily intimidated or bribed into silence and would most likely have melted away into the favelas again before anyone official had a chance to question them.

Medical Laboratories Inc. seemed to be the best lead they had, but their offices and laboratories looked entirely above board on their visit. They might well be the "brains" behind the operation, but was there any chance they would allow themselves to be caught red-handed at any stage? The management had been willing to co-operate under only the lightest of pressure. It seemed likely that the actual criminals were buried more deeply in the system.

"We probably need to watch the premises for a day or two," Julia suggested one evening as they sat in their hotel room with the door firmly locked, chewing their way through yet another room service meal, "see who goes in and out."

"Stake the place out?" Geoff asked. "Couldn't we hire a private detective to do that for us?"

"Would you have any idea how to go about finding someone reliable to do a job like that in this city?"

"Good point." Geoff chuckled, eating another mouthful before pushing the rest of the food aside. "We could go there tomorrow morning. Should we have a camera, do you think?"

"Sometimes, Dad," Julia said, waving her phone at him, "I forget what a total dinosaur you are."

He grinned sheepishly. "Ah, yes, technology, of course."

At seven thirty the following morning, Julia having picked up two coffees and paninis in a nearby Starbucks, they were parked up watching the entrance to the offices of Medical Laboratories Inc.

"Just coffee is fine for me," Geoff said as she offered him the food. "It's a bit early for eating."

Julia took a bite and stared at him thoughtfully. "Are you on a diet or something, Dad?"

"No" – he avoided her eyes – "probably just a touch of traveller's belly."

"Your stomach's upset?"

"It's nothing." He waved her concern aside. "I'm just not hungry."

Julia said no more, eating both paninis herself as the minutes ticked by. The only activity in the street was people arriving for work in the surrounding offices, but there were enough parked cars for them not to be too visible. Julia was enjoying spending so much quiet time with the father who all her life had either seemed to be distracted by other people or away on some important business. It felt good to have had his full attention for whole days on end.

During the first hour or two a number of people went into the door at Medical Laboratories, looking like anyone else arriving for a normal day at work. Julia and Geoff thought they recognised the lawyer who had talked to them, and the girl from reception who had summoned him. Most of the others seemed like regular office workers, but some looked more like medical technicians or possibly even doctors. Julia photographed each of them as they went in. They all arrived individually and on foot, which seemed perfectly normal behaviour for commuters in a big city.

At around ten o'clock a couple of minibuses turned into the road and pulled up beside the door. They appeared to be full of children, although it was hard to see through the tinted windows.

"What's this?" Geoff said, pulling himself up from the semi-comatose position he had slumped into during the wait, "a school outing?"

"They don't look like schoolchildren," Julia said, pointing her phone at the buses as the nervous-looking children, most of them barefooted or wearing flimsy rubber sandals and ragged clothes, were ushered from the vehicles into the premises. "They look more like street children to me."

"They certainly look like they've been living rough."

"So what are they bringing them here for?" Julia wondered out loud.

"I guess they have some time to sell," Geoff said after a moment's pause, his voice grim.

"They're not old enough to agree to that," Julia said, horrified at the thought.

"I doubt they have any idea that's what they're here for. They've probably just been offered a free breakfast."

A battered Toyota pulled up behind the coaches and Julia was unable to stop herself from exclaiming as the driver got out and opened the back doors to allow more children to spill out. "Beatriz?"

Remembering why they were there, she snapped a dozen pictures as Beatriz exchanged a few words with the bus drivers and ushered the children through the door, following them inside.

"Beatriz?" Geoff asked, "The woman you told us about? The one running your charity?"

Julia nodded, unable for a moment to find any words as she struggled to work out what could possibly be going on. She searched her brain for a logical explanation as to why Beatriz would be delivering so many children to a place like this, but the only answers she came up with horrified her.

"Maybe we've totally misunderstood who Medical Laboratories are and what they do," she said eventually. "Maybe it's something totally innocent."

"Or maybe your friend Beatriz has totally misled you," her father suggested. "Is that possible?"

Chapter Nine

The night before they were due to fly back to New York together, Geoff and Julia went to visit Gabriel and Isabella, taking them out for a meal to try and explain what they were hoping to achieve by going back to the US. The young Brazilians were scrupulously polite and grateful, but subdued. It was obvious that they felt the Americans were going to abandon them, just as they felt every other do-gooder had done before.

"We're going to try to fight for compensation for both of you," Julia told them, "and for the other victims. But we have to do that from the US because that is where the company behind the whole testing process is based. You will have to take care because a lot of people will have accepted bribes along the way in Rio, and they are all going to want to silence you and the other victims. Do you want us to arrange to move you somewhere safer?"

"I think there are too many of us for them to silence us all," Isabella said. "We have met so many others at Doctor Amy's surgery, all of us having the same experience. We like to stay in the home we built together."

"Once the company finds out we're after them, the people who stole your time will be looking for ways to get to you," Geoff warned. "They will be willing to pay local thugs, or perhaps even the police, to do their dirty work for them."

"The police don't like to come to the favelas. Only in force," Gabriel added. "We are safer there than in the city centre or even out in the countryside. People will warn us if there are killers looking for us. You go back to America and do what you have to do."

"Just take extra care is all we're saying," Julia insisted. She was pleased to see what an improvement Dr Amy's painkillers had made to their ability to move comfortably and to lead normal lives, but Isabella still became tired by the end of the meal and needed to go home to bed, whereas most women her age would have been fired up and ready to go on somewhere else to dance the night away.

Julia also noticed that her father was pushing the food around his plate as he talked, leaving most of it for the waiter to remove once the others had finished theirs. She assumed his stomach must still be playing up.

The following day Geoff and Julia headed for the airport. Julia was surprised when her father stopped several times to stare into duty-free shop windows on the way through the terminal. He never usually showed any interest in such things.

"Are you looking for anything specific, Dad?" she asked on the third stop.

"Not really," he replied vaguely, "maybe something for your mother."

"What, perfume or something?"

"Something like that."

"You won't find anything for Mum in there," she said laughing, pointing out that it was a store selling trainers and sports equipment."

"No," he said chuckling. "I guess not."

"How about over there?"

Puzzled, she led him over to the perfume counter and they bought a bottle of Carole's favourite. Geoff fumbled with his boarding card at the till.

"Are you OK, Dad?" Julia asked.

"Yes, of course." He sounded defensive.

"Here" – Julia handed her card to the sales assistant – "use mine."

"I must be more tired than I realised," Geoff said as they moved towards the lounge area, and Julia realised that the window shopping had just been an excuse to pause and get his breath back on the long walk to the lounge.

"We have been putting in a lot of hours," she agreed. "We've probably missed a few too many meals as well – and eaten a fair bit of junk."

"That's probably it." He seemed grateful for her explanation for his sudden lack of energy, but she noticed he was still avoiding eye contact with her. "Let's get something to eat before boarding."

His energy levels seemed to lift again once they'd eaten, although he only took a few bites of the sandwich he'd ordered, but several times on the flight Julia thought he looked unwell and short of breath. She could tell she was annoying him by constantly asking him if he was OK, so she pretended not to notice. The walk through the airport at New York was obviously hard for him. By the time they got back to the house he was too exhausted to put up a fight when Carole and Julia told him to go straight to bed.

"I think he needs to see a doctor, Mom," Julia said once Geoff was out of earshot. "He didn't look well on the plane but he won't admit it."

"I told him the trip would be too much for him," her mother said, "but he won't listen to me. You know what he's like about that sort of thing."

"Leave it to me," Julia said, her expression grimly determined.

That night she decided on a plan.

"I've made an appointment for both of us with Doctor Adams tomorrow," Julia told Geoff the following evening as they ate supper.

"What on earth for?" He seemed startled and annoyed at the same time. It was almost as if he felt guilty about something as well as affronted at not having been consulted. Carole kept eating, staring at her plate as if she wasn't listening, allowing Julia to handle the matter.

"Well, we've been hanging out in a lot of crowded clinics the last few weeks. It's quite likely we've picked something up. It wouldn't hurt to get a few things checked."

"Like what?"

"I don't know – blood tests, urine tests, whatever it is doctors do when their patients have been hanging out in slum clinics."

"I don't need to go," he said after a moment's thought. "Cancel the appointment. You go if you want."

Carole looked up from her plate. "Don't be ridiculous, Geoff. Julia's quite right. What harm can it do just to get checked out?"

"Also," Julia pressed her advantage, "you've hardly eaten anything in the last few days and you said your stomach was playing up. It shouldn't be going on for this long."

"Oh, for goodness' sake." He dropped his knife and fork onto the plate with an aggressive clatter. "I see quite enough of that man."

"Who?" Carole asked, alarmed by such uncharacteristic behaviour in her usually calm husband.

"Dr Adams."

"You haven't been to him for years," she retorted. "Or is there something you're not telling me?"

Geoff sighed deeply and neither of the women broke the silence that followed, both determined to force him to open up. Eventually he leaned forward, taking hold of both their hands across the table, and spoke quietly.

"I've been to see Adams a few times recently," he said. "I just didn't want to bother either of you with it until I had to."

"Bother us with what?" Julia asked, glancing nervously at her mother who had turned pale as she stared fixedly at her husband's face, waiting for him to continue.

"They've found a few shadows here and there—"

"Here and there?" Julia's voice came out higher than she expected. "Where exactly?"

He gripped their fingers more tightly. "Pretty much everywhere, actually."

"And what does he think you should do about it?" Carole asked, hardly able to choke the words out of her tightening throat.

"He says there are basically two options. They could chop out most of my insides and shoot an enormous amount of chemicals into what is left. Or alternatively they could just control the pain and let nature take her course."

"Oh, Daddy." Julia spoke softly, sounding almost like she was remonstrating with him for some trivial foolishness. "How long does he think you have?"

"Julia!" Carole was shocked by the starkness of the question, not yet ready to think of such things.

"No" – Geoff squeezed his wife's hand – "it's OK. Julia's right. We all need to know what we're dealing with. I can talk about it now." He took a deep breath. "If they just control the pain, I can probably keep going for another six months or even a year. If they do all the surgical hacking and chemical bombing, they might be able to extend that – although they can't be sure – but I would spend most of that time either in hospital, with tubes everywhere, or in bed recuperating from being in hospital."

"All that time we were together in Rio and you never said a word…" Julia was trying to process the information. "I thought we were spending quality father–daughter time…"

"We were." He squeezed her hand. "It would have been a pretty grim few weeks if this had been all we talked about, wouldn't it? That's why I wanted to come down. I wanted to make one last contribution, and I wanted to spend time with you."

"Why didn't you tell me?" Carole asked.

"Would you have let me go if you had known?" he asked, and she didn't answer. "Exactly. It was what I wanted to do and now I want to stay home with you."

"Do the boys know?" Carole asked.

"Of course not," Geoff replied. "I wouldn't tell anyone before I told you. Adams is the only one who knows anything at all."

"Six months to a year?" Julia was still trying to take the magnitude of the news in. "That's insane."

"You have to tell the boys, Geoff," Carole said, her voice cracking.

"I will. I will."

"I can take over the Yokadus case," Julia said. "You'll need to relax."

"Nonsense." He let go of both their hands and went back to picking at his food as if the subject was now closed. "I want to keep going with the case. Not much point in living if you aren't doing anything useful."

Carole stiffened visibly.

"Just don't write me off yet, is all I'm saying."

"But I want to spend time with you," Carole said quietly.

"We will spend time together," Geoff said. "I can work from home. And I'm going to need your help to raise funds for the battles ahead."

"Of course." Carole took a deep breath and composed herself, knowing that Geoff wanted to change the subject. "I'll do whatever you want."

"Ironic, isn't it?" Geoff grinned at Julia.

"What is?"

"If only I could buy a bit more time."

* * * * *

Geoff made the calls to his sons after supper, and later that night Matt texted Julia: *In Manhattan on business tomorrow. Fancy supper? Just the two of us?*

That would be great, just tell me where and what time and I'll be there, she texted back.

The following evening brother and sister embraced as they arrived at a midtown family-run Italian restaurant, holding onto one another for far longer than either could remember doing since they were children, finding comfort in the embrace before slipping into the secluded booth the restaurant manager had reserved for them. Both had tears in their eyes as they made a show of studying the menus while they composed themselves.

"How long have you known?" Matt asked once they had ordered their drinks and asked the waiter to come back for their food order.

"Just found out yesterday, about half an hour before you."

"He never mentioned it all the time you were together in Mexico?"

"For God's sake, Matt, it was Brazil."

"What?"

"We were in Brazil. Rio to be exact."

"And he never mentioned that he was dying?"

"Not a peep. He was obviously not well but he just said he had an upset stomach from the food or the water or whatever."

"And you believed that?"

"It seemed perfectly credible, Matt, at least to start with, given the sort of places we were eating and going to the bathroom."

"Spare me the details." They fell silent for a few moments. "What exactly was it the two of you were up to down there anyway?"

"It's a case that has caught his imagination – pharmceutical companies doing illegal procedures on people too poor and disempowered to know what they are signing up for – mainly children in fact. This idea of buying time from poor people, shortening their lives so rich people can live longer. Dad feels really strongly about it. As do I."

"Is this the illegal side of the trading-time thing?"

"How do you know about that?" Julia was genuinely surprised that her effete brother would know about anything so sordid.

"I'm a banker, Julia, we have to keep an eye on what's going on around us, keep up with the trends and the research programmes, look for investment opportunities."

"Watching the world fall to pieces from your ivory tower?"

He laughed and toasted her with the glass of whisky the waiter had put in front of him. "Touché, little sister." She raised her martini in a return salute. "To be honest, it is pretty much the only thing anyone in the financial world is talking about, along with cryptocurrencies."

"Really?"

"Why so surprised? A whole new market trading in time? It's going to be huge once it goes legit. At the moment it's just on the Dark Web and stored in mafia warehouses, but it is still making millionaires out of a lot of people. Once it becomes legal, the banks want to be ready to trade in it properly. Most governments want to be involved too. It will be the biggest thing since the Silicon Valley boom, potentially bigger. There are people expecting to become very, very rich on the back of the trades they are doing."

"They are already doing trades?"

"There's a futures market in them. It's always the people who get in early on new things who make the big bucks. At the moment it's all underground, but preparations are being made. But you wouldn't know because you've been deep in the heart of Mexico."

"Brazil, Matt, Brazil!"

"I know." He grinned, and for a moment he looked like the big brother who used to tease her about her Barbies when she was six. She let out a genuine laugh before they both remembered why they were meeting and grew thoughtful once more.

"You talk like you think that is all OK," Julia said.

Matt shrugged. "I think it's inevitable. As long as there is a demand and as long as there are people willing to sell, then the market will emerge. It's a law of nature, a bit like the sex trade."

Julia curled her lip in disgust at the suggestion.

"It's probably better that the whole thing is above board and legal," Matt continued, "so that it can be regulated and the profits can be taxed. If it stays underground, it will develop just like the drugs and sex trades, and all the money will go to the criminals and people will be dying all over the place because it will be going on in back-street clinics with untrained staff."

"That can't be right," Julia protested. "You can't believe that control of something this dangerous should be put into the hands of people like Larry McMahon who just want to please their shareholders and make themselves rich. Dad doesn't believe that and Larry is his oldest friend."

"He'll have to stop all that," Matt said.

"All what?"

"Exhausting himself chasing around trying to save the world. Now he's sick he'll need to rest."

"He'll never do that. If he's only going to live another year, he wants to cram every minute of it with useful work."

"Maybe that's what made him ill in the first place. Is there a way we could purchase him some time from this new facility? You must have met some people who can help. Should we talk to Larry?"

"Matt! Dad would never agree to that, and nor should he. He disapproves of the whole idea and everything about it. Plus, you've just said yourself that the whole thing is still underground and dangerous."

"I'm not suggesting we take him to some back-street clinic in Venezuela. I believe there are some private clinics in California and Switzerland that are pretty safe, but expensive."

"That is exactly what's wrong. Why should it only be people who can afford to fly to Switzerland or Palm Springs who get to live longer?"

"But if he could buy another five years, he might be able to achieve what he wants to achieve. As it is he may not live long enough to see it through. A year is not long in a big corporate case like this with money being thrown at it to deliberately slow things down – which is exactly what Larry and his lawyers will do."

"Maybe having a reason to keep going will prolong his life," Julia suggested. "At least it will give him something else to think about, something more challenging than the approach of the Grim Reaper. Something for us to do together as a family."

"Maybe we could purchase the time on his behalf" – Matt continued talking as if his sister hadn't spoken – "and tell him that it's a painkiller or something. Would that be possible?"

"Are you suggesting we lie to our dying father? Jesus, Matt!"

"It's just a white lie, and if it prolongs his life—"

"No, Matt!" She slammed her fist on the table, making heads turn in their direction. "It's completely against everything he believes in – and everything I believe in, come to that!"

"He's your father, Julia, show some heart! We want to keep him for as long as possible, don't we? We want the kids to know him long enough to be able to remember him once he's gone."

"Don't do this to me, Matt," she warned. "You keep going down this path and you will drive a wedge between us all."

"We've had wedges in this family before and we've got over them," he reminded her.

"I know," she said, "but then we had time to let things blow over. Now we don't."

He spread his hands wide, as if she had just made his point for him.

"Doug agrees with me," he said.

"You two have talked about this already?"

"Of course we have."

"And Doug sent you to win me over? You should both be ashamed of yourselves."

"We just want to keep Dad with us for as long as we can," Matt said, and she could see that his eyes had filled with tears again. For a moment he looked like the boy she remembered who used to come to her for comfort after a telling-off for something from their dad. Before she could respond, the waiter appeared beside them to take their food order.

"You also need to start taking more precautions," Matt continued once the waiter had left and he had recovered his composure.

"Precautions?"

"Security. Personal security for you and Dad and also at the house. If you and Dad have been turning over stones in Rio, you can be certain that the people at the top have heard about it. They will be wanting to shut you up before you start making a big noise and disrupting their trade."

"For God's sake, Matt. This is twenty-first-century New York, not nineteenth-century Sicily."

"Don't be naive, Julia." Matt squeezed her hand so tightly it hurt but she didn't let the pain show on her face. It was a trick she had learned when she was six and her brothers worked so hard to see if they could make her cry. "If you thought about it for ten seconds you would know that I was right. If you were advising yourself as a client, you would be saying the same thing. They will try to get to you, so you need to be prepared."

Chapter Ten

When Carole answered the door all she saw was a giant bouquet of flowers with legs standing on the doorstep.

"Delivery for a Mr Geoff Madison," the bouquet said.

"Larry?" she said. "Is that you? What are you doing?"

"I come in peace." Larry grinned at her round the side of the flowers. "I heard the old boy is poorly."

"You look like a wedding florist!"

"They're beautiful, no?" Larry held the flowers at arm's length as if it was the first time he had really looked at them. "Think he'll like them?"

"I'm sure he'll appreciate the gesture," Carole said, "but who told you he was ill?"

"A lot of people care about him. They want the best for him. I'm his oldest friend. I should be here for him."

He was already sidling into the house, even before Carole had stood back to make room for the bouquet. Outside she noticed his car parked discreetly on the other side of the drive with the driver waiting inside, staring straight ahead, stony faced, his black-gloved hands resting on the steering wheel.

"No helicopter today, Larry?"

"Listen, don't go busting my balls, Carole," he said grinning. "I was just in the neighbourhood."

"You are never *just* in any neighbourhood, Larry." Carole laughed, despite feeling annoyed by the unannounced incursion into a house she was trying to keep calm and restful for Geoff.

"Larry?" Geoff had appeared from the dining room where he had just finished toying with a meagre breakfast.

"Hi" – Larry thrust the flowers at him – "these are for you."

"Flowers? Really?"

Geoff was obviously as unsure as his wife about how to respond to the unexpected appearance of a man he was about to lock horns with very publicly. He took the bouquet and passed it to Carole, who disappeared towards the kitchen, leaving them alone.

"It's a peace offering," Larry said, dusting the pollen off his lapel.

"You want coffee?" Geoff asked after an awkward few seconds of silence, leading the way back into the dining room where the housekeeper was clearing the table. He signalled to her to leave the coffee pot and poured them each a cup. He then walked through the French windows and sat on the patio outside. Larry followed, obviously unsure how to behave in a situation where even he could see his normal bravado and bluster was totally inappropriate.

"So, how are you? You look great. I was expecting to find you stuck in bed with tubes coming out of you."

He was more ill at ease than Geoff had ever seen before. Illness and the prospect of imminent mortality obviously made him nervous. He perched on the edge of one of the chairs, gripping his coffee cup so hard his knuckles were whitening.

"Who told you I was ill?"

"I'm your oldest friend," Larry said again, as if it was a line he had rehearsed many times, baring his teeth in what should have been a smile. "You should have told me yourself."

"I've only just told Carole and the kids. It's not going to make any difference to anything. I might still outlive you, old man, with all the stress you put yourself through."

Larry was taken aback by the suggestion that he too might be mortal. "Well…" he said, obviously wanting to say more but thinking better of it.

"Oh, of course," Geoff said laughing mirthlessly, "you have probably already bought yourself a good few extra years off some poor sod in a slum somewhere."

For a second it looked as if Larry was going to allow Geoff to anger him. His knuckles whitened still further and his eyes narrowed as if taking aim, but he made a visible effort to control his temper.

"Listen, Geoff. Let's not allow this thing to ruin our friendship. Not after all we've done together over the years. Let's leave the fighting to the lawyers, if we have to fight – or maybe just call a truce. If we don't have long—"

"I am a lawyer, Larry, in case you have forgotten."

"Why are you doing this, Geoff? Why do you want to spend your last days fighting in court, waging a war you are never going to see the end of and can't possibly win?"

"Because what Yokadus is doing is wrong. The whole concept is wrong. Poor people shouldn't be persuaded to sell their lives any more than they should be persuaded to sell their bodies for sex or their kidneys for transplants."

"It's the greatest concept for the redistribution of wealth ever," Larry said, fighting the urge to shout. "You or I get to live a few more years and the guy we do the deal with gets to build a house for his family, educate his children, start a business…the opportunities are endless. If he makes some money, he can then buy the time back. It's like taking out a mortgage but using your lifespan as collateral instead of your home."

"It's no good going over the arguments again, Larry. I've thought about it from every angle. I've been down to Rio with Julia and seen the real price these people are being persuaded to pay just so that people like you and me can keep making money for a few extra years. It's wrong, and Yokadus have been breaking any number of international laws to make it happen faster. You have been trading on the Dark Web without any of the necessary safeguards. You have been doing a lot of physical damage to a lot of innocent people. You know all this, Larry. I dare say you think it is a price worth paying for the final result, but I don't believe it is."

Larry fell silent for a moment and both men stared down the garden towards the beach as they gathered their thoughts, their anger festering beneath a veneer of calm which neither of them wanted to take the risk of destroying, knowing there might not be time to repair it later, both afraid of the nuclear cores they might expose.

"All your life," Larry said eventually, "you have worked to build up your firm and take care of your family. You have done an amazing job, everyone knows that – you know that!

Now you are blowing the whole thing up just to prove a point. You must know that if you and Julia are going to persist in this witch-hunt against Yokadus, we won't be able to keep any of our business at Madison's? Even if you are retired and even if Julia were to resign tomorrow, there is no way. I know how big a part of Madison's turnover Yokadus represents. It will be a body blow you won't be able to recover from. Once you are gone your family are going to need an income—"

"The firm will be just fine without Yokadus," Geoff interrupted, keeping poker-faced. "There's plenty more fish in the sea. It was time for some new blood at the top anyway. I have total faith in Julia, Daniel Steinman and the rest of the team. I would like to think that you would not be so petty as to deliberately try to destroy a well-run firm that does a lot of good work in the world."

"If you keep this up, I won't have a choice," Larry snapped and then shut his mouth before any more anger managed to escape.

"Nothing you can say is going to dissuade me from the belief that what Yokadus has done and is doing with this time-trading is morally wrong," Geoff continued in a measured tone that made him sound calmer than he actually felt. "And that what you have been doing in these slums is illegal in virtually every country you have done it in. When I get to the end of my time I want to know that I've done everything I can to stop it."

"Saint Geoff, eh?" Larry sneered, his exasperation finally overwhelming his patience. "Well" – he stood up – "may the best man win." He turned as if to leave and then swung back and stretched his hand out. "I wish you'd let your kids buy you a few more years. None of us want to lose you yet, however much of a pain in the butt you may be."

Geoff clasped his old friend's hand but said nothing. Larry did not release his grip and pulled Geoff's face close to his so that he had only to whisper for his parting words to be heard.

"Don't," he hissed, "at any stage underestimate how far I will go to beat you. Remember that your family will soon be surviving without your protection."

With that he did not look back as he walked around the outside of the house to find his driver, who was still sitting motionless at the wheel awaiting his instructions.

"Are you alright?" Carole asked, coming out through the French windows as soon as she heard Larry's car drive away.

"The boys must have told him," he said. "They shouldn't have done that."

"They love you, Geoff," she said. "You can't blame them for wanting to keep you around a bit longer. Wouldn't you have wanted to keep your father and your grandfather if you had been offered the option?"

A sudden and painful coughing fit prevented him from answering.

Chapter Eleven

"Good to have you back," Daniel Steinman said, giving Julia a peck on the cheek.

"I doubt you mean that," she smiled understandingly, taking a seat in his office without an invitation. It still felt more like her father's office but she knew she was going to have to get over that.

"Well..." he thought for a second "...at a personal level I certainly mean it. From the angle of the business..." He left the thought hanging in the air.

"Yokadus?" Julia raised an eyebrow.

"It became official today. All their business has been moved. We now have quite a few people on the payroll with a lot of time on their hands."

"We can find plenty for them to do," Julia said. "We have a big case to build."

"You are going to be using Madison's to close down time-trading and prosecute Yokadus?"

"Need to keep everyone busy," she joked, unsure what Daniel would say next.

"Who will we be billing for all this work?" he asked after a long, thought-filled pause.

"Us. We will be fundraising. There are a lot of people who feel strongly that this is something that needs to be stopped."

"So you are going to be crowdfunding one of the potentially biggest lawsuits in the world?" The tone of his voice told her that he didn't think that would work.

"I hadn't thought of it quite like that, but in a way I guess so. My mother has always been very good at fundraising for good causes. I think this is the best cause ever and she's certainly on board to help in any way she can."

"The sort of people in your mother's network who donate to causes tend to be the comfortably off," Daniel said, raising an eyebrow to suggest that he was understating the case. "Which means it is possible they're also the people who are most likely to be in favour of time-trading."

"Not all of the one per cent are necessarily immoral and self-serving." Julia spoke sharply, as if personally insulted by his suggestion. "Some of us have consciences and understand the difference between right and wrong."

"Understood," Daniel said quietly, "but you take my point. You may find that the majority of the people you know think differently when it comes to buying a few extra years for themselves and their loved ones. Yokadus has a lot of supporters for this concept amongst the one per cent."

"Crowdfunding from the other ninety-nine per cent it will have to be then," she said laughing, eager to diffuse the tension in the air. She knew she needed to keep Daniel and the rest of the Madison team onside in the coming months because there would be far too much work for her and her father to handle on their own. Daniel nodded thoughtfully but said nothing. "So," Julia continued, "can I count on your support, as long as the money is there to fund the necessary hours?"

"It's bound to be a very high-profile case," Daniel said after considering for a moment, "and your family have always been very careful to keep a low public profile in the past. How does your father feel about this?"

Julia wondered if Daniel had heard any rumours about Geoff's health and, if so, whether that would affect his enthusiasm for taking on the case.

"My father believes one hundred per cent that time-trading is immoral and should not be legalised. We also have evidence that Yokadus has been experimenting on people without their knowledge or full consent and harvesting dangerous amounts of time from them under false pretences and without any of the required licences or tests. He believes we should not allow ourselves to be bullied by threats of uncomfortable levels of media exposure. If that is the price we have to pay for doing the right thing, then we should gladly pay it. We will also be willing to fight fire with fire – hiring our own media experts."

"Yokadus has very deep pockets," Daniel warned, "and I imagine Larry McMahon is taking this all very personally."

"He's my godfather," Julia said with a shrug. "It would be hard for him not to take it personally because it is personal. My father is one of his few real friends and has been his lawyer for pretty much all his business life. None of us are going into this lightly."

"So who, exactly, is our client?" Daniel asked.

"My father is the client and we will work to get as many high-profile people on the team as possible. We need celebrity firepower."

Daniel wrinkled his nose at the thought of becoming part of the celebrity media circus but nodded his understanding. "It seems like a cause worth fighting for," he agreed eventually. "Let's do it."

"I told Dad we could count on you," Julia said, standing up and blowing Daniel a kiss before heading to the new office she had been allocated since her return to work.

As she walked through the panelled corridors, past portraits of her ancestors, she was mentally compiling a list of calls she needed to make before the end of the day. The bandwagon was now rolling.

* * * * *

The first call was to Lucy Phelan, Jake's wife, who Julia had known for most of her life. She knew that Lucy, tired of waiting for her husband to come home each evening, had returned to her career as a corporate communications consultant. Before her marriage she had been communications manager for one of the biggest players in Silicon Valley; now she had her own consultancy in Manhattan, with several of Jake's companies as her clients. She had started it as a partnership with two other women she knew from her Silicon Valley days and the consultancy was now part of a network of international agencies.

"Are you free this evening?" Julia asked, once the preliminary niceties of the call were over. "There's something I want to talk to you about, but it will take a bit of time to explain. I thought perhaps dinner?"

"I have a book launch this evening at The Pierre," Lucy said. "Why don't you come to that and we can eat afterwards."

"Perfect."

The launch was for a new cookbook by a celebrity chef and Julia spent half an hour kissing the cheeks of people she vaguely knew from school, or through her parents, and sipped champagne through the speeches as she waited for Lucy to decide it was safe for them both to leave.

"Shall we eat here?" Lucy asked, and a few minutes later they were sitting in the hotel restaurant, Perrine.

"Somebody told me you had gone off to South America to be a nun or something," Lucy said once they had ordered salads and a bottle of wine.

"Hardly," Julia laughed. "I went to Rio to work in the favelas for a while."

"To see how the other half lives."

"I guess, although it's more like the other ninety-nine per cent."

"Ah" – Lucy raised her glass – "am I hearing the sound of the guilty conscience of the one per cent?"

"Not quite how I would put it" – Julia raised her glass in response – "but perhaps it contains an element of truth. Do you know much about Yokadus?"

"Larry McMahon's company, isn't it? Pharmaceuticals and stuff? Isn't he a buddy of your dad's? Jake worships him."

Julia took a deep breath and started from the beginning. Their food arrived but it was some time before either of them picked up their forks. Lucy was transfixed and kept asking questions. Eventually, when Julia had finished, Lucy speared a mouthful of salad.

"That is so weird," she said, "because I know for a fact that Jake has been trading on that market, and sampling the goods himself."

"He's been buying himself time?"

Lucy nodded. "You should see him. He looks twenty years younger."

"Does he want to buy some for you too?"

"He's never suggested it." Lucy made a wry face. "I suspect he's thinking he will be trading me in for a younger model before long anyway, so there's little point in him prolonging my life."

"Lucy!" Julia was shocked by the seriousness of her friend's suggestion. "Where's he ever going to find another woman that puts up with him like you do?"

"Please, Julia, he's an adrenaline-fuelled billionaire, he could have his pick of the young Russian models who hang around in all the places people like him go to."

They laughed, although they both knew she was not entirely joking, and ate in thoughtful silence for a few minutes.

Finally, Lucy pushed away her plate and sat back, nursing her glass of wine. "So, basically, you want someone to put your side of the case to the media?"

"I'm guessing that Larry is going to throw everything he has at painting Yokadus as the good guys here," Julia said, "so we need to get in there and tell our side of the story first. I am also guessing that he will want to spin the case out for as long as he possibly can. We have good reasons why we don't want that to happen, so I want to put pressure on Larry to make him realise he needs to sort it out quickly before Yokadus's reputation suffers any more damage."

"Can I ask what your 'good reasons' for wanting a quick solution are?"

"I'd rather not say at the moment." Julia was smiling but her voice was stern enough to put Lucy off probing any further. She had no intention of sharing her father's illness with anyone until she had to.

"Would you like me to put together a proposal?" Lucy asked.

"I would like that very much."

They touched glasses and Julia went into more detail about her experiences with Gabriel and Isabella and the patients at Dr Amy's clinic.

Chapter Twelve

Geoff wasn't sure how he would feel going back to the offices of Madison and Partners as a client, a place he had spent more waking hours in than any other, including his home. He was pleasantly surprised to find that he didn't feel any pangs of regret at no longer spending every day of his life there. Now that he had confirmation that his stay on earth was limited, he actually wondered why he had allowed his clients to take up so much of his valuable time over the years, but he knew it was too late for any regrets now.

It was obvious that Daniel and the other partners were keeping the firm going in exactly the way he, his father and his grandfather would have wanted, and he was painfully aware that they must be struggling financially following the loss of the Yokadus account.

"You look well, Geoff," Daniel said as he ushered his ex-boss into the office that had been his for so many years. What he was actually thinking was that Geoff had lost a shocking amount of weight since leaving the firm and seemed to be moving as slowly as an old man. The collar of his tailor-made shirt now looked several sizes too large for his neck and his suit hung off him like it had been made for a man twice his size.

"Retirement must suit me," Geoff replied. He had blocked all thoughts of being ill from his mind, determined to continue enjoying whatever time was left to him and definitely not wanting to waste any more time discussing it with anyone else. The trip into the city, which had once been his daily routine, had left him exhausted. A fact he was determined to keep to himself.

"I gather from Julia you have been keeping yourself pretty busy and you're coming back now as a client."

"It's likely to be a very high-profile case," Geoff said. "In the long run it will bring in a lot of business, more than enough to offset the loss of Yokadus. But I'm aware it will change the nature of the company. Madison and Partners has always had a reputation for being low key and discreet. Some might even say 'stuffy'. Neither my father nor my grandfather would have wanted to take on a cause that would get us splashed all over the front pages of the press, but times change and probably the firm needs to reflect that."

"I'm told that these days we have to worry more about what gets said on social media than in the newspapers." Daniel smiled as he poured them each a coffee.

"Well, I think like an analogue dinosaur and that pretty much illustrates that we needed to make some changes around here." Geoff laughed. "I'm not going to pretend I wanted to retire when I did, Daniel, but I can now see that it might have been the right time for someone younger to take the helm, someone who better understands the way the world is going. I could have hung on for another ten years, but there is a danger I would have blocked the way for younger, fresher minds."

"I think you are being unduly modest, Geoff. I don't think there are many people who understand quite so well exactly how things work as you do. But I agree, it may be time for Madison's to become a little more high profile to attract new clients. It would also seem that morally and ethically we're on the right side of history with this case. The public mood is turning against the way the rich are hoarding their money, and worries about the growth of the wealth gap are very high on the agenda of most young people, right up there with climate change and the destruction of the environment. We could come out of this case in a much stronger position than we go in." He paused for a significant time. "As long as there is still enough money to pay the wages while we're fighting it."

"Carole and Julia are dealing with the fundraising. I don't think it will be a problem."

"They will make a formidable team," Daniel agreed.

"Quite." Geoff opened his briefcase and took out a bulky file. "Since I am, whatever you may be kind enough to say, a bit of a dinosaur, I've printed copies of all the evidence we found in Rio, but I will also email files across to you. This is just what Julia and I found out in a few weeks of digging and it is only Rio. I'm quite certain that Yokadus, or their representatives, have been illegally stealing time from people all over Africa,

Asia and South America, doing the most terrible amount of damage to their victims and then just disappearing and taking no responsibility for the mess they leave behind. It is like the Opium Wars all over again. I think once we start publicising this case, others will come forward."

"Like the #MeToo movement."

Geoff thought for a second. "Yes. That would be a pretty good model for how it would work. It takes a few people to have the courage to stand up and speak the truth and then others will feel safe to come forward with their own stories."

"We just need to make sure they know to come to us," Daniel said.

"I knew you would be the right man for this." Geoff laughed and dropped the file on the desk between them, pleased to be rid of the weight of it. "Let's put a stop to this whole sordid business."

* * * * *

When he got home that evening he found Julia staring out at the garden, obviously agitated.

"Problem?" he asked, sinking into a chair with a relieved sigh.

"I don't know. Lucy is doing a great job of raising media interest in Gabriel and Isabella. I want to let them know that there are going to be journalists knocking on their door. I don't think it is fair to spring it on them without warning. I rang Maria Morales to ask her to go round and tell them. She hung up as soon as she realised it was me."

"You think she knows anything?"

"About Beatriz being involved? I don't know. Maybe she's involved too. If she is, then she will have worked out that Gabriel and Isabella are our star witnesses." She turned and looked at her father. "You don't think we've signed their death warrants, do you?"

Chapter Thirteen

Gabriel first heard about the film crew that was looking for him from a group of excited small boys on the street.

"They're asking where to find you," the boldest of the group told him. "We said we would find out for them."

"Did they pay you well?" Gabriel asked.

"Sure," the boy said grinning.

"Good for you," Gabriel said laughing and ruffled his thick hair. "Find out more about who they are and what they want and then maybe we can set up a meeting."

The boys scampered happily back towards the hotel where the film crew had told them they were staying and Gabriel returned to the task of helping Isabella to get up and dressed. Some days the doctor's painkillers worked better than others, and that morning they didn't seem to be having any effect on the stiffness of her joints or the weakness of her muscles.

"How do we know they are a genuine film crew?" Isabella asked as he gently washed her face. "They could have been sent to kill us."

"I will look after you," he said. "I promise."

Once he had her settled in her chair, she smiled up at him but he could see the fear in her eyes. She had seen the gun that he had bought and hidden under their mattress when he thought she was sleeping. She knew exactly how much danger they were in.

When there was another knock on the door two hours later, Gabriel assumed the boys were back with news. Instead he found a strong-looking American woman with a small backpack slung over her shoulder. Behind her he could see a man with a camera around his neck and a bulkier backpack.

"Hi, Gabriel?" the woman asked.

"Yes," Gabriel replied cautiously. Behind him Isabella reached over from her chair, sliding her hand under the mattress until she felt the reassuring weight of the gun.

"Hi, I'm Kate. I'm a friend of Julia Madison's."

"Julia?" Gabriel couldn't work out what was happening. Any friend of Julia's was obviously welcome in his home, but who was this woman and why was she there, with a photographer?

"Can we come in?"

Gabriel nodded and stood back to let her in.

"Do you mind if he takes some shots?"

The photographer followed, not waiting for permission, and immediately started taking pictures of the room and of Isabella, hunched in a chair, apparently sipping innocently at a chipped cup of coffee, one hand still under the mattress. When she looked up it was easy for the photographer to capture how beautiful she had once been, before her cheeks had sunk in and her teeth had worked loose. The eyes were still the same perfect shape, but filled today with pain rather than joy.

"I'm a journalist," Kate was saying as Gabriel put a reassuring hand on his wife's shoulder to calm her. He could see she had found the gun and he wanted to restrain her before she did something rash. "Julia wants us to tell your story to the world so that we can bring the people who did this to you to justice and make them pay for their crimes."

"You want to hear our story?" he asked.

"I would love to hear your story," she said, settling herself on the floor and extracting a small recorder from her bag.

Kate was still there, asking questions, when the street boys came back from the hotel with news that the film crew had also mentioned Julia's name and they were in Rio to make a documentary about Dr Amy's patients and the stories they had to tell.

"It seems you are going to be world famous," Kate said. "Julia asked me to give you this." She handed over a small parcel. "It's a phone. Julia says use it for whatever you need. It will be paid for from America."

* * * * *

At the same time as Lucy Phelan was building up the media profiles of the people who she wanted the world to see as the victims of time-trading, the communications department at Yokadus, and the consultancies they employed most regularly, were working to find stories about worthy recipients of extra time. In private they had to admit that it was not the easiest of tasks.

"High-net-worth individuals are hard for the average Joe to sympathise with," one communications strategist admitted during a presentation to Larry and his board of directors, "so we need to concentrate on the good work that people can do if they are allowed to live a few extra years. There is a doctor in his seventies who still works ten hours a day travelling around India, performing operations that save the sight of small children. He's willing to admit that he has bought himself another ten years, which means many thousands of children who would have gone blind if he wasn't able to help them, will now be able to see."

"Fantastic," Larry barked. "That's exactly the reason why we have to save this project from the wreckers."

"Indeed," the strategist agreed, "but there are very few cases that will play that well with the public. Most of the people who are willing to admit to being buyers are also heavy users of Botox and spend more time in front of mirrors, doing yoga or working out in the gym, than they do saving the sight of penniless kids. We think it is better to play on the benefits to those who might otherwise be bereaved. Most people can identify with a kid who doesn't want to lose a beloved grandparent—"

"Or a parent, even," Larry butted in again. "Everyone feels sympathy for orphans, right? All of us would like to keep dear old Ma and Pa around for a few extra years."

"Exactly. But timing is crucial here because the 'wreckers', as we may well call them from now on, are already getting their stories out there. We can't risk spending too much time searching out these true stories. We need to put together an advertising campaign now and script some dramas that everyone can identify with, using actors."

"You mean throw money at the problem?" one of Larry's fellow directors said.

"I think we should do that," Larry talked over her. "This is what it's all about. Kids deserve to have their families with them for as long as possible. If people can extend their lifespans, we can get back to multigenerational families – Grandma helping out with feeding the kids, Grandpa taking them fishing. It's a great concept."

"For God's sake, Larry," the director snapped back, "you think the public are going to swallow that? Multigenerational families are a necessity in the Third World and if people are selling off their time, kids from poor backgrounds are going to have shrinking families not growing ones. They will actually be losing their parents and grandparents earlier than they otherwise would have done. It'll be a repeat of all those kids left behind by the AIDS crisis in Africa."

"But overpopulation is one of the biggest causes of poverty," Larry carried on, becoming more enthusiastic for the idea the more he thought about it. "Too many mouths to feed in families with scarce resources. We can help with that problem too. It's a win-win."

The director closed her eyes as if despairing of everything that was happening in the room around her. Larry pointed at the strategist. "Get your creative people to come up with some storyboards."

The film crew that Lucy Phelan had persuaded to follow up the story in Rio spent several days with Gabriel and Isabella and other patients at the clinic before turning their attention to covertly watching Dr Beatriz Sanchez and Medical Laboratories. They rented a room opposite the premises and set up twenty-four-hour surveillance through one of the windows. On the fourth night the cameraman who was taking the late shift smelled smoke. By the time he had woken his colleagues and alerted them to the danger, the fire had taken hold of the old dry timbers of the building. All of them managed to escape through the windows but none of their equipment could be saved. The following day the road was cordoned off by the police and the public were informed that the buildings were unsafe because of fire damage. When the director of the film insisted he should be allowed through to see if there was anything to be salvaged, he was politely told he could not. When he continued to insist he was arrested and put in a cell. His colleagues were taken straight to the airport.

Chapter Fourteen

The first attack on the Yokadus factory took everyone by surprise, from Larry and Geoff down to the two security guards who had worked there all their lives and had never had to do more than check people's passes and make sure all the locks and cameras were kept in good working order.

It happened a few weeks after the airing of the news item about Gabriel, Isabella and the other patients at Dr Amy's clinic, and the exposure of Medical Laboratories, Dr Beatriz Sanchez and the mysterious fire which had almost killed an American film crew – and had led to the imprisonment of the documentary's director and a high-profile campaign by his family who were demanding his immediate release.

"This is getting us far more coverage than the actual documentary would have done," Lucy explained to Carole and Julia at their daily meeting. "We don't have to ask people to sit down and watch an hour of television on one selected channel – they are hearing the story on every news bulletin on every channel, whether they choose to or not. It's spreading like wildfire."

Kate's article had come out in print first and had flamed across the internet. The news item about the film crew had then been widely covered in the press and the televised reports had started to trend on YouTube in the form of sound bites which had been selected by Lucy and her team for their ability to shock and to move people. A large proportion of the world's population was indeed shocked to discover that time-trading was even a thing, let alone something that was creating scores of new millionaires amongst speculators, and that someone was willing to kill and imprison journalists who tried to expose the story. Those who had been aware of it were now having to think about the moral dimensions more deeply than they might have done previously, and those who already knew that they were uncomfortable with the concept of time-trading were given, in Yokadus, a target upon which to focus and vent their anger.

People writing on the subject in the media led to questions being asked at governmental levels and then to protests in streets from Washington to London and Paris, Rio to Freetown. The demonstrations started as good-humoured affairs, celebrating all the positive things in life, but within a few days they took an uglier turn. The language on the posters and in the chants of the crowds became angrier and more violent and then unidentifiable figures, their faces covered by scarves, began to hurl missiles at the police and hide behind hastily constructed barricades. It wasn't long before the more authoritarian governments ordered the riot police in with baton charges and water cannons, which caused the anger levels to rise still further.

The people with scarves became people in balaclavas wielding clubs, and rather than going out onto the streets and then becoming angered by the reactions of the authorities, small groups began to plan attacks on particular targets. The batons and water cannons of the authorities were replaced first with rubber bullets and then with live ammunition. Because of the exposure that Lucy and her colleagues had orchestrated, the most obvious targets for the protestors to go for were Yokadus, PSG and Medical Laboratories. The first attacks on each happened on the same night.

Seeing how many headlines the attackers received, activists in a hundred other countries publicised the names and addresses of medical facilities they believed were harvesting and storing time illegally, as well as companies trading locally with Yokadus. Even those who were conducting perfectly legal and ethical business found themselves tarred with the same brush as those who were shown to be linked with organised crime. Anyone with a link to Yokadus was assumed to be doing something immoral, even though most of them were not.

"Larry must be having to hire an army of security people," Carole said as she and Geoff read the morning papers. It was taking Geoff a little longer to get going in the mornings and he was still in his pyjamas, even though he had been making phone calls for several hours. "It must be causing him a lot of pain on the bottom line."

"Not enough to stop the project," Geoff replied. "He predicted it would be the biggest money-spinner of his career and he's not wrong. It's possible that if he wins this case, he will be the richest man on the planet within a couple of years."

"But that could change, right?" Carole said. "If people stop wanting to do business with Yokadus because of the bad publicity, things could start to go wrong."

"His share prices are already falling, but they could rise again just as fast," Geoff said. "However, if we can get the government to ban the trade, then all the billions he's anticipating making, and no doubt borrowing heavily against, will evaporate overnight."

"Poor old Larry," Carole sighed. "It's hard not to feel sorry for him."

"The longer he carries on trying to push time-trading through the legal system," Geoff said, "the more damage he will potentially be doing to the rest of his interests. If he wins the case and they make it legal, he will make so much money he will be able to recover easily. If he loses, then it could be the end for the whole company."

"You don't have to feel guilty about that, Geoff," she said, squeezing his hand. "He was willing to wipe Madison's out as well."

"I know," Geoff sighed, "but it doesn't feel good after we spent so many years helping him to build Yokadus up from nothing. A lot of people are bound to lose their jobs."

* * * * *

The fall in the share price, the hiring of security guards and the building of fences around every Yokadus location were only a few of the ways in which Geoff and Julia's campaign was costing Larry money. The advertising campaign that had started in the US had been rolled out around the world. In First World countries, where the majority of customers for time-trading were likely to be found, the creative people developed the idea of small children being able to spend longer with their beloved older relations, adding in worthy case studies as they found them of doctors, teachers and scientists who could extend the longevity of their socially productive careers by purchasing extra years.

In poorer countries the admen sought out stories of ambitious young people who were able to turn round their own lives, and the lives of their children and grandchildren, by sacrificing some of their own time, making both the decision and the process look like selfless, joyous events. They showed houses being built and successful businesses being launched with the money earned from selling time. Happy families celebrated piped water and air conditioning coming into their homes, and big family meals were filmed with tables covered in food and drink, surrounded by happy, laughing faces. The ads showed grateful families hugging and thanking the people working in the clinics for allowing them the opportunities to send their children to school and university for the first time ever. Each ad carried a disclaimer to assure the viewers that they were imagined scenes because no such trading had yet started. Because of Lucy's simultaneous public relations campaign, few people were fooled by such declarations of innocence.

Determined to stop the trade at any costs, the more fanatical activists also started targeting the advertising agencies and law firms that worked for Yokadus, necessitating increased levels of security around offices in virtually every big city.

"We seem to have set off World War Three," Daniel mused on a visit out to Oakdale as he pushed Geoff's wheelchair down the garden to the beach.

Geoff had been forced to confide in Daniel that his time was running out to stress the urgency of reaching a conclusion to the campaign, and at the same time admitted that he was finding the trips into Manhattan increasingly tiring and wanted to ration his energy for the things that mattered most. Daniel was happy to take time to travel out of town to the pleasant surroundings of Oakdale for meetings, most of which Carole and Julia also attended. He was struck by how happy the family seemed to be working together on a project they all believed in so strongly, their dedication and optimism masking the fact that Geoff was obviously growing weaker every day.

Chapter Fifteen

The moment Julia realised she was being followed on her morning journey to the office, she felt mixed emotions. It was certainly frightening to sense someone's eyes on her, knowing that they were always there, no matter how many corners she dodged round, but at the same time it was exciting. She actually felt ridiculously flattered to think that anyone thought she was important enough to waste their time on.

Her first reaction was to tell someone, but something made her hesitate. If she told Daniel or one of the other lawyers, they would insist she did something about it, like call the police, and for some reason she couldn't explain she didn't want to frighten her tail off until she knew more about what they wanted. Was she being rash she wondered as she settled herself behind her desk, remembering her brother's warnings about hiring security. Now that the story had gone public, she believed the chance of meeting an untimely death had receded, but what if someone was waiting for an opportunity to kidnap or intimidate her in some way? What if they still wanted to kill her as a warning to their growing band of enemies? There had been a lot of violence breaking out at Yokadus facilities – what if someone had decided to take some retributive action?

She pushed the idea aside, telling herself that if that was the case, they would have pounced by now. If they wanted her dead, then it would not be hard for a company as rich and powerful as Yokadus to arrange for a car accident. What was she thinking? Larry was her godfather; he would hardly order her execution. Would he?

Someone came into the office with a question and distracted her as she engaged her brain for the day's work. It was not until she went out for her regular midday jog in the park a few hours later that she remembered what she had been thinking about. Normally she would have put on earphones and listened to music as she ran, but this time she decided she needed to keep all her senses alert.

Coming out of the building, she jogged on the spot for a moment, looking casually around as if undecided about which way to turn. She could see no one behaving oddly, so she set off in the same direction as always. Two blocks later she came to the park and realised that she was doing exactly what people in this situation are always advised not to do: she was following her usual route. If someone was watching her, they would know that it was likely she would be running here at this time. Had she subconsciously done that on purpose, she wondered, to draw her stalker out in broad daylight?

She was not the only runner in the park, but most of the faces she passed doing their stretches looked familiar. It seemed that she wasn't the only one who liked to stick to a routine. No one looked to be watching her, so she kept running. Everyone was travelling at different speeds; some she overtook and others would streak past her. After one lap she sensed that one particular man seemed to be keeping pace with her, just far enough back to be out of her eyeline. She tried speeding up but he was still there, just a metre behind her. She slowed down and he did the same. Her heart was thumping now and she didn't think it was because of the exercise.

"Don't turn around," a man's voice said. "Just listen."

He stopped talking as a young athlete went past them both, only speaking again once the woman was out of earshot.

"I have information on Yokadus that will help you but if they find out I've talked to you, they will kill me."

"What information?" she asked, staring straight ahead as she ran.

"If you want to know more, take breakfast at the Pershing Square Diner tomorrow morning. Come on your own. Get there at seven. Tell them you are expecting to be joined by someone and ask for a booth."

Before she could say anything he sprinted away and she had no chance to see his face before he left the park.

For the rest of the day she had trouble thinking of anything else. It was exciting, like being part of a movie. She didn't feel in personal danger; after all, the man could have attacked her in the park if he had wanted to, and she knew Pershing Square Diner well. It was directly opposite Grand Central Station, a huge bustling place with plenty of staff. She was confident she would feel safe there. The hardest thing was not telling anyone about the assignation, but she knew that if she mentioned it to anyone else in the family, they would insist that she did not go alone, and she was sure that her contact would not join her if he suspected there was anyone else there. The idea of not finding out what he had to say was unthinkable.

At seven the next morning she was waiting outside the diner for the staff to open up the doors. She tried to stop herself from constantly looking around at every passing face, attempting to look like any other worker by staring at her phone, checking her messages and emails. After what seemed like an age the doors were opened and she made her way in with a few other early birds.

"Can I take a booth?" she asked the waiter who led her through to the main room at the back. "I'm expecting someone to join me."

"Sure." He directed her to one of the plush red leather booths raised up on a platform along the wall, looking down on the rest of the tables. It would definitely be harder for anyone to overhear anything they might say than at one of the tables on the open floor. "Can I bring you coffee?"

"Please. And orange juice," she said, studying the menu as she sat down, forcing herself not to look around at the other early diners.

The waiter returned moments later with the drinks. "You want to order or wait for your friend?"

"I'll order," she said. "A fresh fruit bowl and eggs Florentine."

"Of course." The waiter disappeared again, leaving her alone with her phone.

The fruit bowl arrived and other tables began to fill up as commuters poured in from the station and night workers stopped by for a meal before heading home. The place ran like clockwork, the staff used to serving people in a hurry. The eggs

Florentine arrived within minutes. She was not used to eating such a big breakfast and the adrenaline rushing through her system made it hard to swallow, but at least the food meant she fitted in with everyone else.

"More coffee?" the waiter asked, refilling her cup almost before she had time to reply.

"Thanks."

"Sure. Is everything OK with your breakfast?"

"Great, thanks."

"Sure."

The moment he moved away, a man slid into the booth opposite her and picked up a menu. The waiter swivelled, startled by the speed with which the man had arrived.

"Hi, welcome. Can I get you coffee?"

"Yes, please," the man replied without looking up, and the waiter filled his cup.

"The eggs Florentine are good," Julia said, pointing at her half-eaten plate.

"I'll have that," the man said.

"Sure," the waiter replied, "coming right up."

"Good morning," Julia said once they were alone. "This is all very dramatic."

"I work for Yokadus," he said, not wasting any time on small talk, "on the Yokadrix-C project."

"Is that what they call it?"

He didn't reply.

"What do you do for them?"

"I am an accountant," he said. "I was brought in from one of their other companies. I've been with them all my working life. I can't afford to lose my job. I have kids and I will need my pension, but I don't believe that what they are doing is right."

"OK. So what is it that they are doing that you want to tell me about?"

"Trading-time illegally. Initially I accepted the company line. I could see that if poor people could make some seed money by selling a few months of their natural lifespan, then it would help alleviate poverty and transfer capital to the people who need it the most. I actually thought it was a pretty neat idea. A game changer for closing the inequality gap."

"But you've changed your mind?"

The waiter was back with another eggs Florentine, which he placed in front of the man. He neither acknowledged its arrival nor picked up his knife and fork. He simply kept his head down and waited for the waiter to go again.

"Can I get you guys anything else?" the waiter asked.

"We're fine for the moment," Julia assured him. "Thank you."

"Sure."

"They transferred me to a top-secret installation in Utah," the man continued once they were alone again. "None of your protesters have found it yet."

"They're not exactly *my* protesters," she said laughing, but he didn't even smile. He was obviously terrified and wanted the conversation over as quickly as possible.

"They are stockpiling the time that they are collecting from volunteers all over the world – mostly from the poorest African and South American countries. They have been doing it illegally for several years, taking way more than they are telling people. The idea is that by the time it has all become legal and people are used to the idea of buying time, Yokadus will hold the biggest store in the world. No rival companies will be able to catch up. It's like having one private bank owning all the gold bullion in Fort Knox. They will then be able to manipulate the price as demand increases or supply diminishes.

"If there is a danger that the market is getting flooded and prices are going to drop – which is probably what would happen if it were allowed to operate as a completely free market – then they will simply destroy the stockpile and all those poor people will have sold their time with no benefit accruing to anyone except Yokadus shareholders."

"So Larry is planning a financial fraud on top of the ethical questions?" Julia said, almost to herself.

"I've been thinking about it a lot," her informant continued, his food still untouched. "I still don't know exactly how I feel about the ethics of time-trading, but I do understand the ethics of market manipulation, monopolies and price-fixing. What they are planning is illegal as well as immoral."

"What are you hoping I will do with this information?" Julia asked.

"I think the best way forward is for people to be told about the facility in Utah. You could let the relevant people know. If they can penetrate the security, they could get the data out and pass it to someone in the media who will know how to make it public before anyone has time to stop it."

"Let the relevant people know? Who are the relevant people?"

"The media or the people who have been attacking other Yokadus facilities."

"I'm not running a guerrilla army," she said.

"I understand," he said, without looking up, "but you could make contact with someone who is."

Julia allowed herself a smile as she realised that she probably could do that. It was the first time she had seen herself as part of such a radical movement.

"Where exactly is this facility and how would someone gain access to the premises and to the data?"

He slid a piece of paper across the table and she immediately pulled it down onto her lap. "That has the address and also all the codes needed to get through the security doors and to access the relevant files."

Without another word he stood up and left the diner.

"Everything OK?" the waiter asked, pointing to the untouched food.

"Sure," Julia said. "He was called away urgently. Can I have the check, please?"

Chapter Sixteen

Julia, Lucy and Carole were brainstorming at The Pierre the following evening, Geoff having admitted that he needed an early night and insisting that he didn't need babysitters with him every hour of the day.

"If we're going for another round of fundraising," Carole said, "then we have got to offer people something new, something really special. You can't just keep on asking for more money, especially from people who have already given generously."

"I've been thinking," Lucy chipped in, "could we bring Gabriel and Isabella up to New York, or maybe even tour them around a few places?"

"If they were guests of honour at a dinner and told people their story, I think we could raise a lot of interest," Carole agreed, and turned to her daughter. "Would they be up to it, do you think?"

"Maybe," Julia said, "if we looked after them every step of the way, made sure they got plenty of rest. I was planning to go down to visit them anyway, so if they are up to it, I could bring them back with me."

"I think that would be great," Lucy said, "but I wouldn't want them to feel that they are being exploited all over again."

"We could make it the trip of a lifetime for them," Carole suggested. "God knows, they deserve it."

"I'll call them this evening," Julia said. "If they like the idea, then we'll sort out whatever they need by way of visas."

She was having trouble concentrating on the conversation, constantly glancing at her phone, waiting for a text. She had made several phone calls when she got to the office that morning, still buzzing from the excitement of her breakfast liaison, and eventually she had found someone who wanted to listen but who didn't give her a name. She told him there was a piece of paper with all the relevant information on it. She asked if he wanted her to text the details to him.

"Definitely not," he said. "Go about your normal business. Keep it with you. We will get in touch."

"Have you got a date or something?" Lucy asked, catching Julia looking at her phone yet again.

"No!" She realised she had answered too quickly, sounding too defensive, making Lucy and her mother exchange knowing looks. "I haven't. I'm just waiting for someone to contact me."

"Sounds like a date to me," Lucy teased.

Julia's phone vibrated and she saw the text. *Take a toilet break.*

"I'll be right back," she said, standing up and walking quickly to the toilets before either of the others could decide to come with her. A sudden rush of adrenaline made it hard to breathe and she felt strangely light-headed.

One of the cubicles was shut and another woman was adjusting her make-up in the mirror. She was young and smart looking. She glanced across at Julia and nodded towards the cubicle, putting a finger to her lips. Her purse was standing open on the vanity unit beside her. The woman gestured towards it with her eyes and Julia dropped the piece of paper into it before walking into another cubicle and shutting the door. She sat down and waited until her heartbeat had returned to normal and the person in the other cubicle had left. By the time she came back out the girl had also vanished.

*****

If Yokadus knew that their security had been breached and their data hacked, they didn't inform the media. The first the outside world heard about it was when an investigative journalist released the information two weeks later. Within a day the facility in Utah was ringed by vans and tents as protesters set up camp, their placards demanding that the Department of Justice arrest Larry McMahon and close down the facility.

"They won't arrest him, will they?" Julia asked her father as they watched the television news together.

"Not at this stage," he said. "At the moment it's just a slogan, but it is good to keep this on the agenda. Someone did a good job getting those details out to the media."

Julia didn't take her eyes off the screen. She didn't think her father, or anyone else, needed to know the part she had played in the leak.

A month later, she was back in Rio to collect Gabriel and Isabella and couldn't resist going to the PSG offices in the centre of town on the way. The windows had been boarded up following attacks with bricks, and there were heavy locks on the doors that someone had obviously tried to smash off, perhaps homeless clients hoping to find shelter in the abandoned offices. For a moment she felt a pang of sorrow at the thought of all the well-meaning volunteers who she had got to know during her time there. She hoped that they had found somewhere else to direct their energies. There was a note pasted to the door that gave several addresses and telephone numbers for other services that people could go to if they needed them. Maybe, she told herself, everyone who had worked there had found other charities to offer their services to.

Maria's office in the favela was still open, although all the PSG signs had been diplomatically removed. Julia knocked tentatively on the door.

"Yes?" Maria shouted impatiently from inside.

Julia opened the door and poked her head round. "Hi, Maria."

"Oh, it's you," Maria said, and looked up from her paperwork. "What do you want?"

"I just wanted to see you and say hi."

"Well, here I am, no thanks to you."

"I'm sorry..." Julia came further into the room, despite feeling deeply unwelcome. "I'm sorry that this has had such a bad effect on PSG, but it wasn't right what Bea was doing."

"What do you know about right and wrong?" Maria spat. "You come down here from your fancy New York life and you decide what we should all be doing? You think Bea is bad because she was helping kids make some money? You think she didn't weigh up all the good against the bad before making her decisions? You think it is all so easy to stay on your high moral horse when your family is hungry?"

"No." Julia felt like a naughty schoolgirl being hauled in front of the headmistress.

"So now a lifetime's work is over for her and the kids are still on the streets, still hungry, still having no schools to go to, still getting into the drugs trade, still getting killed. But you, you are sorry! So that is OK."

"It's not right for the poor to have to sell their time on earth to the rich," Julia said, realising that her intellectual argument sounded weak beside Maria's heartfelt fury.

"Nothing down here is right, you stupid girl," Maria shouted, "but a lot of people were trying their best to make it better and you have put a stop to that. Just get out of my sight!"

Aware that nothing she could say could carry any weight against Maria's years of hands-on experience of poverty and inequality, Julia was forced to leave the room with a heavy heart, struggling against the self-doubts now swirling around inside her head, aware that blood was rushing to her face in a mixture of anger and shame.

Gabriel and Isabella were waiting for her in their house. They were both excited but Isabella already looked tired from the effort of getting up and dressed.

"You will be able to sleep on the flight," Julia assured them as she helped them out to the car with their small, carefully packed bag.

Lucy was waiting at JFK in New York for them with a bank of photographers and an airport buggy so that they could be whisked through customs and immigration without having to expend any more energy than strictly necessary. The adrenaline surge of the journey seemed to have energised both of them and they happily posed for pictures as they were whisked down the seemingly endless corridors towards the full glare of the fundraising publicity machine.

Chapter Seventeen

"This is your room," Carole said, leading a wide-eyed Gabriel and Isabella into the main spare bedroom at Oakdale. "We thought you would be more comfortable here than in a hotel, and it will be more private."

The room had views down the garden to the ocean beyond. The windows were open and a light breeze was stirring the long silk curtains. The whole room was furnished in greys and creams, calming their souls and bringing tears of pleasure to Isabella's tired eyes. For a second it felt like she had actually died and arrived in Heaven.

"The bathroom is here" – Carole opened a door on to a cream-tiled wet room with a large free-standing bath in the centre – "and there is a coffee machine and fridge with a few cold drinks so that you don't feel you have to keep coming downstairs and asking for things if you would prefer to be private and rest. Having said that, do please feel free to come down whenever you want. Please use the house and the garden as if they were your own. The ocean is a little cold for swimming in, but it can be very nice and peaceful on the beach, and there is a swimming pool that is a little warmer.

Just let us know if there is anything you need. We plan to have supper in a couple of hours."

She had given similar welcoming speeches to many hundreds of guests over the years, but never before to anyone who was struck totally dumb by the loveliness of her home. It was a pleasure for her to see it through the eyes of someone new, a couple who had never before stayed in such a comfortable house. They were obviously totally overwhelmed by the whole experience. The bed looked so smooth and perfectly made that neither of them wanted to crease it with the weight of their bodies, the carpet was so pristine and soft they were frightened to walk on it for fear of leaving footprints, even though they had already pulled off their shoes and walked through the house barefoot, marvelling at every painting, ornament and soft furnishing that they passed.

"I see you don't have any luggage," Carole said as she backed towards the door, eager to give them a chance to be alone and catch their breath, "but I believe Julia is sorting you out some clothes, so don't worry about a thing. You are the most important people in the house at the moment and we want to make you as comfortable as possible."

As Carole closed the door behind her Isabella walked over to the window and slid cautiously to her knees, painfully aware of all her aching joints as they sank into the thick pile of the carpet. Leaning on the sill and resting her chin on her arms, she closed her eyes to feel the cool breeze on her exhausted lids.

"I always dreamed that we would have a room like this one day," she said as Gabriel sat down beside her. "It's so beautiful. Like in the magazines."

"Julia and her family are being very kind to us," Gabriel said. "Without them none of this would be possible. Who would have thought that we would ever travel first class on an airplane?"

"Or drink champagne and eat food like that?" Isabella giggled and for a moment she sounded like the young girl he had first fallen in love with.

He held her tightly and they both watched the wind moving the trees around the old garden and wished they could enjoy the pleasures of the day in the same carefree way they had enjoyed their first days together when they had needed nothing other than a future together.

Julia had to wake them a couple of hours later to give them the clothes she had bought for them and to tell them there was a meal ready downstairs in the kitchen if they felt like it.

"Dad is really looking forward to seeing you again," she said. "He hasn't been well and you will notice a big difference in his appearance."

When they reached the kitchen they were shocked to see how much Geoff had changed since they last said goodbye to him in Rio. He was already sitting at the table and he was dressed, but his shirt collar now looked several sizes too big for him and his cheekbones had risen from the dry, falling flesh of his face. He opened his arms to embrace each of them but did not attempt to stand. Even though Julia had warned them, they were still not prepared for the physical evidence of his decline and Isabella was unable to stop tears coming to her eyes.

Lucy was hovering in the background, nursing a large glass of white wine that Geoff had gone to great pains to choose for her from his collection. She had always enjoyed visiting Oakdale ever since she was a little girl, but watching Geoff from across the room, a man who had always seemed such a tower of strength when she was young, was giving her pause for thought. Her own father was older than Geoff and although he was still in robust health, spending large parts of his year either skiing or playing polo, Geoff's obvious mortality was making her think about how long it was likely to be before he too started to show signs of reaching the end of his life. That led her on to think about her mother, a woman whose lifelong hypochondria had led to none of the family ever taking any notice any more when she complained of headaches or digestive disorders and assured anyone who would listen that they were being caused by the arrival of life-threatening tumours. One day, Lucy reflected, her mother would be right and there actually would be something wrong with her, and one of her symptoms would be genuinely life threatening. She wondered if she would be able to resist the temptation to encourage them to buy some extra time from someone like Yokadus. She gave a shiver and took a large swig of wine before obeying Carole's instruction to pull up a chair and eat.

"I hope you didn't mind all the photographers and cameras at the airport," Julia said to Gabriel and Isabella once they were all eating. "We feel we need to get as much publicity as possible while the media are still interested in your story. They can be distracted so quickly by new stuff."

"It was nice," Isabella smiled shyly, "like being a film star for a day."

"What you are doing is really important," Geoff said, "and we're very grateful to you for coming all this way. We may not be able to stop people from trading in time in the future, but we can at least make sure that the legislation and medical guidelines are tighter around the whole area so that people don't end up being tricked into selling too much time by ruthless operators like Yokadus."

"When I first realised that Isabella was becoming so old so soon because years had been stolen from her," Gabriel said in a voice so grave everyone stopped eating for a moment to listen, "I thought it would be OK because I would find a way to make some money and buy time back for her. I even made enquiries—"

"And what did you find out?" Geoff asked.

"I found out that I would need ten times as much money as we had been paid to buy enough time to get Isabella even halfway back to how she was before we walked into that place."

"And then," Isabella cut in, aware that Gabriel was choking up with emotion, "we talked about it a lot, and we talked to other patients at Doctor Amy's clinic, and we realised that even if we did buy some time back, we would be taking it from someone else, putting them in the same position that we were in. It made our consciences ache to think of doing such a thing."

"That's such a lovely way of putting it," Carole said, discreetly blowing her nose. "I wish more people would be guided by an 'ache in their conscience' instead of letting greed and fear of death guide them."

She placed her hand across her husband's where it lay on the table, squeezing it reassuringly.

"There's nothing for me to be afraid of," Geoff said, "because I've had a relatively long and totally wonderful life. I have three beautiful children and four beautiful grandchildren. I've served my purpose."

Lucy had pulled out her phone and pressed the record button, keen not to forget any of the conversation she was witnessing, imagining how she could use these words to touch the hearts of the outside world.

"You have plenty of money," Gabriel said, blushing at his own boldness in speaking up. "If you bought just a little time, you would have more years to help others by fighting this thing."

"Everyone can find some justification as to why they deserve to live longer," Geoff said, "but I'm no different to you two or any of the other patients at Doctor Amy's clinic. Who knows what you would have achieved in the years that you have had stolen from you?"

"We know people in our neighbourhood who have bought time," Gabriel said. "They are not good people. They are the ones who sell drugs and run prostitutes in the favelas. They are the only ones with the money to be buyers, not sellers. They think we are stupid for being the ones who sell, and now I think perhaps they are right."

"You absolutely are not!" Julia pounced on his words, making him jump. "That is exactly why the whole idea is morally wrong. It is the ruthless people and the bullies and the cheats who become the richest people in any society, and they are bound to be the ones to benefit from this, never the people who truly deserve to be given more time on Earth.

"Yokadus are running all these ads around the world, suggesting that sweet white-haired old grannies will be staying longer with their loving and devoted families, baking apple pies and dispensing love and wisdom, but those are never going to be the sort of people who can afford to buy time."

"And if they are such sweet old ladies they wouldn't want to take time away from lovely young people like Gabriel and Isabella," Lucy joined in, becoming fired up by the rhetoric.

"You can understand why people would be tempted to buy time, though," Carole said wistfully, "if they have the money and there is someone they don't want to lose prematurely."

Now it was Geoff's turn to squeeze her hand, and for a moment they all fell silent, concentrating on their food and trying to straighten out all the conflicting ideas and emotions that were racing through their heads.

"Since we started publicising this issue" – Julia eventually broke the silence, talking directly to Gabriel and Isabella – "people have been bringing us evidence of all sorts to help us build our case. Some of it is scientific. We have had people who have been working for Yokadus realising that it is wrong and telling us everything they know in exchange for guaranteed anonymity. Some of the stories we have heard are more circumstantial. The media exposed the fact that the corporation has built a vault deep underground in the centre of the State of Utah where it plans to store millions of 'man years' of time, available to trade as soon as the price gets high enough. If the market were to become flooded and prices were likely to drop, then they are planning to destroy those supplies to force them back up again. That means they will be wiping out thousands of years of human life simply to make a bigger profit."

"It is the equivalent of murdering millions of people by bribing them to make the ultimate sacrifice," Geoff added, "which makes it potentially the biggest planned genocide of all time, and they are undertaking it in full view of everyone, including the world's judicial systems, who should be the ones putting a stop to the whole business. I don't know how the activists got to hear about it, but when they did they managed to infiltrate it and copy huge amounts of data from their computers, which they passed to the media."

"Yokadus are pouring a huge amount of money into their propaganda campaign." Julia took over again as she saw her father growing tired from talking as well as sitting up at the table, and also wanting to distract him from thinking any more about how the activists had got into the Yokadus facility and managed to steal the data. "They have been buying advertising space to make people think that what they are doing is perfectly normal and acceptable, to stop people from questioning the ethics or asking too many questions about how it will develop in the future. We know from experience how effective blanket advertising can be. Marketing people have basically shaped all our tastes today. If it hadn't been for them, we would not be spending billions of dollars on cigarettes and alcohol every day, or stuffing ourselves with fat and sugar."

"Big business has become Julia's particular whipping boy for all the ills of the world," Carole said, wanting to stop her daughter from riding too far on her hobby horse since she guessed that Gabriel and Isabella were already losing the gist of what they were having explained to them, however much they might be smiling and nodding their heads in apparent agreement.

"Well," Julia took a deep breath, understanding why her mother wanted her to slow down, "I'm not saying every marketing man is the spawn of the devil, but marketing has certainly been a tool used by many for achieving bad things."

"I don't really understand what you want us to do," Isabella said.

"A lot of people have heard your story," Lucy said, stepping in, "and it has touched their hearts. When they see what Yokadus has done to you, they are more easily able to see why it is wrong. We want you to help us by allowing us to tell more people your story, and by making them realise the real price that is being paid by the sellers of time we will get them to support our cause."

"You want them to give you money?" Gabriel asked.

"Money is certainly helpful," Julia said, "because Yokadus has a lot and it is hard to fight them without some of our own – well, you already know that better than I do from your own experiences in the favelas – but it is ultimately public opinion that we want to influence. A lot of people think only of the benefits for those who are able to afford to buy time – mainly because that is what Yokadus is making them think – and they don't think about it from the point of view of those who are being talked into selling it, young people like you who believe they are being given a chance to make something of their lives when in reality they are being given just one more handicap in the race."

"But you have made your film and written your articles," Gabriel said. "What more can we do?"

"The film was destroyed, although we did still achieve a lot of publicity on the back of it," Geoff said. "Now we need to keep the pressure up while we are building our case to put it before the supreme court. Carole and Lucy here have organised events to raise money and awareness and it would be great if you could talk at them, tell your sides of the story.

"We need to explain that the logical outcome of trading time is that people in wealthy nations, who already live much longer than people in developing nations, will be able to live for ever, while the poorest people of society will end up shortening their lives even further in the pursuit of a dream or a quick buck."

He paused to cough and to recover his breath but no one filled the space and after a few moments he continued.

"Yokadus are arguing that the exchange of wealth for time is morally defensible, that the price of time will be very high and the rewards for the sellers will be enormous. They are saying that quality of life is far more important than quantity. They will argue that the price of one year of time will equal a lifetime of earnings for the poorest of people, and claim that that is defensible. Well, you've already found out for yourselves, the maths doesn't work.

"Two-thirds of the world's population live below the poverty line. Yokadus will pay peanuts for poor people's time and sell it at massively inflated prices, yielding vast profits for wealthy shareholders, who of course will be amongst those who will live for ever, while their donors die, out of sight, in some faraway country."

Geoff continued: "The poor will never become rich selling their time. They will simply disappear. Yokadus will be acting as God, deciding who lives and who dies. They will argue that, for the first time, the poor have a valuable product to sell to the rich, and that somehow this will create a new balance of power in society. This might be true if time were a scarce resource. But, with six billion people in the world, it is not a scarce resource. Yokadus will argue that they can control abuse of the technology by dictators, terrorists, the Mafia and rogue international traders. I can tell you now that based on my forty years as a patent lawyer and expert in intellectual property, this technology is so simple to copy that millions of 'man years' will be stolen and traded illegally across international borders. It will become the new tool for international terrorists and rogue states, replacing the cryptocurrencies drugs, weapons and all the traditional worst excesses of the Dark Web.

"Imagine prisoners in jails ageing prematurely and not knowing why. Imagine children being bred simply for the purpose of trading their time."

The effort of talking for so long with so much passion overcame him and he was silenced by another bout of coughing.

"I wouldn't be able to talk like that to a crowd of people," Gabriel protested. "I would not know the words to say."

"I will write the speech for you," Lucy said, "using your own phrases like the 'ache of your conscience'. That was great. Then you can either read the speech out from a screen or you can start talking off the tops of your heads. It's up to you."

"We can't read," Gabriel said, and they both lowered their eyes in embarrassment.

"Not a problem," Lucy assured them. "We will give you earpieces and I can be feeding you the lines if you dry up.

We'll practise first, don't worry. Whatever happens, people are going to be on your side because they will know the backstory before you have to stand up in front of them. They will be there because they want to hear what you have to say and because they want to help in any way they can. We will make sure everything is filmed for the news channels and social media, but we will also be arranging interviews and handing out copies of the speech to the media afterwards. I promise you we will make it as easy for you as possible and it is your chance to make a really big difference to the future of the world."

* * * * *

That night as they lay together in the luxury of the Oakdale spare bedroom, Gabriel and Isabella hugged each other tightly, unable to sleep despite the comfort of the mattress and the softness of the sheets and pillows, due to a mixture of excitement and trepidation at the responsibility they felt was being put on their already exhausted shoulders.

Chapter Eighteen

Julia and Lucy went to a great deal of trouble to find clothes that Gabriel and Isabella would be comfortable in at the first and biggest of the events, which would also have the desired effect of making them attractive to the media. Lucy spent several days working on the speech that she wanted them to deliver together in front of the audience and, more importantly, in front of the cameras. They had run through it a couple of times and practised with the earpieces, which had left Isabella so exhausted and tearful both times that Julia even considered cancelling the whole idea. When she suggested it to Gabriel and Isabella they were horrified and she could see them dragging up every last ounce of energy they had to fulfil what they now saw to be their obligation.

Geoff was so determined to show them support that he had agreed to be taken to the venue at the Plaza Hotel, even though that now involved him being pushed most of the way in a wheelchair.

The publicity from Gabriel and Isabella's arrival at the airport had already gone viral and touched the hearts of millions. Their story was now well known and being discussed everywhere. A great many people were willing to pay to see them in the flesh and to hear their words. Not only had every seat inside the hotel ballroom been sold at exorbitantly high prices, but crowds of protestors and supporters had begun to build up in the street outside from the middle of the afternoon. To begin with it was a well-behaved mob of serious-minded people brandishing banners, but as the sun began to set behind the high buildings, a noisier and angrier element emerged to populate the growing shadows on the pavements. These were the same people who had been attacking the Yokadus facilities and other locations. These people covered their faces with scarves, wore dark glasses and pulled their hoods up, making them seem all the more threatening in their anonymity. They cheered louder than the rest of the crowd as the diners started to arrive and it sounded more like battle cries than encouragement or approval. Julia felt a shiver of fear run through her when she thought how she had linked herself with these angry, aggressive people in her quest to expose Yokadus, wondering if she had allowed herself to become tainted by the mentality of the lynch mob in the process.

Carole and Lucy had managed to recruit a glittering crowd of guests. There were celebrities to attract the cameras as they twirled and grinned their way up the red carpet and into the hotel, basking in the flash of the cameras and the sounds of their names being called out by fans and cameramen. Then came the New York society figures to bulk out the donations and the bidding at the auction, which was to be held later in the evening, more sedate in their diamonds and furs as they hurried past the crowds, looking neither to left nor right, ignoring the chanting and cheering.

The marketing department for Yokadus was well aware of what was happening and were hard at work putting out counterarguments across social media. Both television viewers and internet surfers were being bombarded with messages about the joys of extended lives and the many good things that could be achieved for the poor of the world with the money that they could earn by selling small portions of their lives. To many they seemed like very reasonable arguments.

*****

Larry had been shocked by the exposure of the data from his facility in Utah and was growing increasingly uncomfortable at the way in which the Madison family seemed to be gaining the moral high ground in public opinion. If he was absolutely honest, he felt in his heart that his old friends had betrayed him and he truly didn't understand what he had done wrong. The messages that his marketing department were disseminating seemed to him to be compelling common sense and he was at a loss to understand why so many people disagreed so violently. Why could they not see that he was offering the entire world's population a chance to improve their lives?

To make matters worse, his young wife had left him after the shortest marriage of his life, giving no real explanation before she went. She had already been spotted in clubs with a much younger man, dancing with a vigour that Larry knew he could no longer match. His normally robust ego was feeling bruised and vulnerable.

He asked to be shown live pictures from the event at The Plaza as they appeared on the internet, and when he saw his old friend being pushed through the crowd in a wheelchair, a frail shadow of his former self, he fell uncharacteristically quiet and thoughtful.

"Such a waste," he muttered. "One phone call and he could still extend his life by years." For a moment he felt an urge to reach out to Geoff and try one last time to convince him of the benefits of time-trading, both for his own self-preservation and for society in general. He even took out his phone and brought up Geoff's number, but he didn't press call. Ultimately, he knew his old friend too well to believe that he would ever betray a principle just to save his own life.

Apart from anything else, the sight of Geoff in the wheelchair was a painful reminder of his own age and of how, if it were not for the extra years that he had bought from his own vaults, he too might be in the same position by now, being a prime candidate for a stroke or some other stress-related illness.

"How can such an intelligent man not understand the benefits that we're bringing to the whole world with this?" he asked out loud, but there was no one else in the room to answer him. "They can't possibly win this fight."

*****

Inside The Plaza, dinner had been served and cleared and Gabriel and Isabella had been escorted to the microphone. With Lucy's voice occasionally whispering prompts in their ears, they talked of the hopes and dreams they had had when they set out that day to the clinic. Gabriel talked of the things he had dreamed of doing for his family with the money, and Isabella talked about how quickly she had found her body ageing and how rapidly all hope of ever being a mother disappeared. Gabriel took over again and talked of how he had wanted to save her by buying back some time but had realised that he could never afford it, and explained that what had been done to them was morally wrong.

The audience rose to their feet at the end, applauding and crying and more than ready to open their wallets when celebrities started to walk onto the stage to conduct an auction of promises. The generosity of the crowd in bidding for the various lots was exceptional, but then many of them had guilty consciences that they wanted to soothe, because they had already been tempted into buying Yokadus's product. They already believed that they had a chance of living for ever. They were already safe, and from that safe position they could clearly see that Yokadus had done wrong and needed to be stopped before things got out of hand. If the process could be stopped these same people would be able to maintain their position at the front of the race, and knowing that weighed heavily on their consciences.

Chapter Nineteen

By now the Supreme Court case of *Madison v Yokadus* had garnered international publicity. Geoff and Carole had watched as the story of time-trading and the issues surrounding it had unfolded across the world, radically dividing opinion between those who supported it as a way of redistributing wealth, and therefore power, and those who saw it as the ultimate example of exploitation of the poor by the rich. Everyone could see the potential benefits that such a massive transfer of wealth could achieve, but most people could also see the potential abuses that could happen as a result. There were some thinkers and commentators who claimed that extending their own lifespans was the last thing they wanted to do, but in most people's hearts there seemed to linger a longing to postpone their personal end and to extend the number of useful years in which they might experience more, enjoy more and achieve more. It seemed that for many people there was an evolutionary longing to get a little closer to immortality, whatever moral sacrifices that required them to make. If men and women could postpone death, perhaps indefinitely, then that meant they had the potential to become gods, which many found a tempting prospect.

Feelings had grown stronger; the more people thought about it and the more they discussed it, the more inflamed the arguments became and the more polarised people's positions. Like abortion, euthanasia, animal rights or climate change, it had become one of those subjects that evoked ferociously strong opinions in some people, while others could see both sides of the argument and were unable to make up their minds as to whether it was the greatest step forward mankind had made since the creation of antibiotics or the worst since the building of the atomic bomb. Those who felt most violently on the subject had started to band together and to form societies whose goals were to insist that the authorities made the process illegal, while others had lobbied the lawmakers hard, claiming that it was a matter for individuals to decide for themselves and that the lawmakers should not interfere in something that should be a free choice. People argued that it was the same as allowing people to choose if they wanted to sell their bodies for sex.

In the lead-up to the supreme court hearings there had been marches in most of the world's capital cities, the biggest happening in Washington itself. Some of the marches ended in violent clashes between the two sides and with police forces sent in by the authorities to control or crush the unrest. Inside the banks and financial markets, preparations had already been made to create a mechanism for the effective trading of time between those who possessed it and wanted to sell it, and ways to store it for those who were fearful of running out of it and who wanted to buy more than they had been allotted by nature. It was no longer a matter simply for individuals to discuss and agonise over; governments also had to decide where they stood on the matter. In the poorer countries of the world they needed to work out how they were going to incorporate it into law and whether they had a duty to protect their citizens from exploitation or to help them to develop the trade and gain fair prices. In the richer countries they had to work out if they were going to put ethical restrictions on the rights of their citizens to extend their lives at the expense of others.

The heart of the debate, however, centred on Washington. If the supreme court decided that time-trading was unethical and made it illegal, that would affect the market in every other country. The first ethical bridge to be crossed by the lawmakers was whether time-trading should be allowed at all. If permitted, the next matter for lawmakers and medical professionals to consider would be how to control the experiments on humans and ensure their safety. Animal rights activists, however, argued that the boundaries had already been crossed if time had been taken from some animals and donated to others, where neither side had the ability to give permission for the procedure.

*****

The Supreme Court Building is as imposing as its architect intended it, reflecting the seriousness of the institution itself, a building of dignity and importance. Geoff was determined to walk up the majestic steps to the plaza on his own legs, even if he had to rely on Carole and Julia for support on either side.

He firmly believed that everyone has a day that defines their entire lifetime, and this, he knew, was his. A number of people, including his family and Daniel Steinman, had tried to persuade him to allow other, younger lawyers to do the heavy lifting for him and speak on his behalf, but he wanted to be sure that the words that went down in the history books were the ones he had chosen and rehearsed a thousand times in his head. He knew that he would never again have a chance to stand up in court and fight for something he believed in so strongly and he was determined to have this one last day for himself.

He had done all he could to convince the world of the dangers of time-trading. Now he just needed to convince men and women who were more eminent and much wiser than him that he was right and Larry was wrong. He was willing to accept that their judgement would be right for the people, regardless of what he personally believed. The great system of democracy had brought him there and he was grateful for that. He would abide by its decision, even if he disagreed with it. If he won this case then the thousands of victims would be able to come forward and sue in the civil courts for compensation for the damage that had been done to them. He might not be able to stop time-trading indefinitely, but he could certainly slow down its progress significantly, see that these people were looked after, and ensure that the right safeguards were put in place for the future.

Lucy had hired a number of extra public relations minders to keep the media at bay upon his request. He did not want to be distracted from the task in hand by barely thought-through questions from journalists who were eager for no more than a catchy sound bite.

Whatever the outcome of this supreme court case, he knew that things would never be the same again.

The justices sat behind a raised bench which was made, like all the other furniture in the stately courtroom, of rich Honduras mahogany, carved from trees that were capable of living anything up to three hundred and fifty years and crafted into furniture which might last four times as long or more. The attorneys arguing the case before the court occupied the desks in front of the bench. When it was their turn to speak they would address the bench from the lectern in the centre. The media were seated on red benches along the left side of the room, already watching the players coming in, listening for clues as to where the story would be going that day.

Larry was already in the room, surrounded by his enormous legal team. Knowing the cameras would be there, he had taken extra care with his appearance and looked thirty years younger than his real age. The two men exchanged nods of unsmiling recognition as Geoff shuffled his way slowly to his seat on the arms of his wife and daughter, much like two boxers touching gloves before the bell signalled that they should come out of their corners fighting.

Geoff was called to speak first. Summoning every ounce of remaining strength, he hauled himself slowly to his feet, watched by a silent room, and took his oath before stating his case, leaning heavily on the lectern and pausing frequently to catch his breath with a terrible rasping sound rumbling through his chest.

"Justices of the supreme court I present myself here today with a very heavy heart. The decision before you is a momentous one, far more significant than anything that has been before this court since its foundation in 1789. Your decision in this case will have far-reaching consequences. The impact will be felt not just in the United States of America but in every corner of both the developed and the developing world. I pray that you are well-guided in this matter. The essence of the reason why we are here today is that you must decide whether one individual's lifetime is more important and more valuable than another's, whether anyone's lifetime can morally be traded nationally and internationally as an investment vehicle and as a commodity. Are we to allow the creation and destruction of lifetime itself by men and women? It is no less a question than can we allow mankind to replace God?

"Let me summarise the evolution of Yokadrix-C and its associated haematological system. I will also try to create a picture of where this technology will take us in the future, if we allow it to develop in the way that Yokadus would like."

He glanced across at Larry, whose expression was a fixed and unreadable stare.

"Yokadus Corporation, who will defend this case, developed a system for the extraction, transfer, preservation and, by default, the destruction of human lifetime. Anecdotal evidence suggests that Yokadus is well advanced in the development of artificial lifetime, far more developed than they would have been if they had followed the letter of the law during the period of testing and development. These 'man years' will be bought from the poorest in society and will be available, if we allow it, to be sold to the most fortunate and wealthiest in society. Here in the United States of America and elsewhere in the developed world, Yokadus will establish a 'time exchange', details of which were recently leaked to the media.

"As you are no doubt aware, there have been huge demonstrations in every major city in the United States since details of the Yokadus technology were first published. The American people have made it clear they do not want this. The rest of the world does not want this. Development of this technology is being funded by a tiny minority in our society who are already living charmed lives and cannot bear to accept their own mortality, at any price."

There was no one listening in the court, or via the media, who was unaware of how close to the end of his own life Geoff was as he gasped for enough air to continue. Knowing that he was a man who could easily have afforded to buy time but had chosen not to, intensified the gravity of his words and deepened the respectful silence in which they were heard all over the world.

"As you will be aware, Yokadus Corporation is currently subject to a temporary injunction restricting it from trading in time. But we have evidence to prove that Yokadus has broken laws in several countries in its relentless pursuit of this technology and the profits that they believe it will produce for them. The power and wealth of those who have the most to gain from this process have enabled it to find its way to legal loopholes that have brought society to the brink of moral collapse. Yokadus is ready to launch this despicable product – in fact, it already has launched it, albeit surreptitiously and illegally. It has already destroyed lives and nothing bar a decision from this supreme court will be able to stop the organisation from continuing to do so, on a massive scale.

"We must never allow them to trade in time and, in due course, we must build into the American Constitution safeguards to ensure that this activity is never allowed to develop in the future. The world is watching us today and I appreciate that the weight on your shoulders requires superhuman strength and wisdom. But the supreme court of the United States of America has never failed its people in the past and I'm confident that you will make the right decision today. May God be with you."

The room remained silent and all eyes followed him as he took several deep, rumbling breaths before shuffling back towards his seat. Geoff Madison had just succeeded in transferring the monkey that had been on his back for so long to the justices seated before him, and the solemn faces of those justices clearly acknowledged that fact. He felt curiously light-headed, even his exhausted body felt lighter; the ordeal was over as far as he was concerned. It had become someone else's problem. He was free to leave the courtroom now, but he sank back into his seat, staying to listen to what would be said next and mustering all his strength for the journey back to Oakdale.

Yokadus put forward Joe Ferero, a smart, confident young attorney who had graduated first in his class from Harvard, and Larry continued to watch the proceedings with an unreadable expression.

"Justices of the supreme court," Joe began, clearing his throat and flamboyantly shooting his snowy-white cuffs out of the sleeves of his five-thousand-dollar suit, "Mr Madison is right about one thing. Yours is a momentous decision. But that is where the veracity of his argument ends. Everyone in this room will agree that science is a wonderful thing, and mankind has successfully dragged itself from the cave by exploiting scientific discoveries and applications, and by the acceptance of new ideas, ways and behaviours. We have trusted the scientists to do right by us and they have served us well over and over again, allowing us to live longer, healthier and safer lives than any previous generation.

"But Mr Madison would like to stop the world just where he sees it. If he had been born a hundred and fifty years earlier, he would probably have prevented the development of the internal combustion engine. If he had been born fifty years earlier, he would have protested about the idea of transplanting human hearts, and all the other advances in modern medicine because, as he sees it, not everyone in society would be able to afford to enjoy these developments. He's a socialist, and socialists do not believe that anyone should have anything unless everyone can have it at the same time. Perhaps he is even a communist – a believer in a system which we all know has been thoroughly and repeatedly discredited by history.

"Mr Madison believes in equality in its purest and most perverse interpretation – if everyone cannot have something, then no one should have it. Following his logic none of us should eat our next family meal until we are sure that everyone is eating as well as we are. He does not argue with the science, the integrity of the process that Yokadus has spent many years and many billions of dollars developing. He does not suggest that it is a danger to human health – because he knows it is not. Therefore he falls back on the moral argument of right versus wrong. The man who says we must not act as God takes on the role of God himself. I assume that Mr Madison does not have a problem with blood transfusions. If so, he was fortunate not to have been born a Jehovah's Witness.

"There are many examples in history where misguided moral positions have flown in the face of common sense. The supreme court of America must make its decision in this case on the basis of common sense and promotion of the common good. The technology developed by Yokadus Corporation is a credit to the achievements of the scientists of the United States of America. Far from creating an imbalance in society and the world, it creates an opportunity to rebalance society. The poor will feel empowered again. They can extract a very fair price for a commodity which they own as a birthright, just as they have been able to sell their manual labour or their ideas in the past. That commodity is not gold or land or property or shares either earned or inherited. It is a commodity that every human possesses. For once, the poor in society can gain a leg up onto the ladder of opportunity. Time that has been sold is not gone for ever. The successful management of funds generated by selling the commodity of time will create sufficient wealth for donors to buy back the time they have previously sold and more. Just as they would expect to have to borrow money to start a successful business or buy a family home, an ambitious young person can temporarily sell a little time to get a good start in life, a start which they would never get any other way.

"We in Yokadus have built sufficient safeguards into the Yokadrix-C system to prevent inflationary or deflationary pressures from upsetting the world market. This is the right course of action for America and for the world. To deny mankind this opportunity for achieving greater equality is to deny mankind science itself.

"Yokadus is already subject to many restrictions imposed by other organs of the state which ensure that our practices are well regulated. The FDA, for example, has imposed two hundred and fifteen restrictions on how Yokadus should execute this technology, but nevertheless the FDA had the wisdom to allow us to proceed. If you must impose more restrictions on how the science is applied, then do so, but for the love of God, don't stop progress here today. Mr Madison has the right, like every citizen of this great country, to seek the opinion of the supreme court, but, whatever he might believe to the contrary, his opinion does not reflect that of all American citizens. The people want progress. Change is what made this country great, and if you decide to inhibit innovation, science, progress, change, whatever we choose to call it, then we will redefine what we are and we will no longer be the leaders of the free world.

"To approve this technology means that Yokadus, a highly regarded American company, would control it simply because it got there first. Not to approve it would simply result in handing over the technology to other people in other countries where you have no control. With due respect to the justices of the court, there is only one right decision here and that is to allow a great technology to advance and further free the world from poverty and inequality, and to give mankind its first shot at immortality. Yokadus Corporation rests its case and may God grant you the wisdom to make the right decision."

Chapter Twenty

The supreme court was due to hand down its verdict three months after hearing the presentations, and the entire Yokadus operation was gearing up to launch their product officially. Larry's lawyers were confident they were going to win and advised him to make the necessary preparations since they were sure rival companies would be quick to take advantage of the market opening when they saw it. Larry agreed with their assessment and hundreds of millions of his dollars were being invested around the world to have everything ready on time.

The last vestiges of Geoff's strength had finally left him as soon as he returned home from the courthouse, having expended every last ounce of the energy he had been storing up for that day. It was as if his body had been holding out until this moment and felt that it could do no more. Now every atom of his being just wanted to rest. He knew that he did not have long to go before the struggle was over and he was at peace with that knowledge and with the knowledge that he had done everything he could to influence the future in the way he believed to be right. If the decision of the court went against him, he would be happy to have left this world before he heard the bad news.

Despite the exhaustion which overcame him, however, his heart continued to beat, pumping the blood round his fragile body, and his lungs continued to pull breath in and out. The doctors managed to alleviate most of the pain and each morning he found himself awake again but unable to summon the strength to even sit up without assistance. The days turned into weeks and then eventually months, and still he found himself waking in his own bed, albeit less often.

Uncomfortable with being a burden to Carole, however much she might protest to the contrary, he asked to be moved to a bed in his study where he could receive twenty-four-hour care from trained nurses without disturbing his wife's sleep or unduly invading her privacy. It was a comfort for him to be able to see his bookshelves and the view out on to the garden through the French windows every time he lifted his eyelids. Carole spent the majority of her days sitting quietly with him. She had ceased talking about the case on the day after he returned from the supreme court.

She knew that this was the day the decision would be handed down, but she did not mention it to her husband when she bent to kiss his forehead as the duty nurse woke him and gently lifted him onto more pillows to ease the coughing. She assumed that he had no idea what day it was. Julia and her brothers had all come home to be with him that day, although they were not quite sure what their role would be.

As they waited, Julia passed the time going through her emails, both the supportive and, to put it mildly, the unsupportive ones. The IT guys at work had installed a sophisticated filtering system that kept out the worst abuse, but some still succeeded in wriggling through the net. She had grown used to it. The case had opened her eyes to an aspect of human nature she had been shielded from during her upbringing, and had taught her how to handle revelations which would previously have knocked her faith in her fellow man. She still appreciated the web for its power and its ability to disseminate information, but she had come to realise that she must tolerate its weaknesses to enjoy its benefits.

The occasional text messages were also drifting in from close friends and associates, even though she had changed her number again the previous week in preparation for this day. Everyone who was important in the context of the supreme court's decision had been notified that a resolution was now imminent; all the others could wait.

It was a surreal feeling to know that the day would either culminate in extreme joy or deep mourning, or perhaps even a combination of the two. Her phone alarm went off at 2.55 p.m. – although she didn't need it since she had been watching every second tick by – and her heartbeat increased rapidly. She left the study to join her mother in the living room. Not a word was spoken. The volume on CNBC was low.

In stark contrast to the calm within the ancient walls of Oakdale, the drama in the air outside the Supreme Court Building was palpable. The media were everywhere. Protesters for and against the decision intermingled. Scuffles were breaking out between rivals holding up placards and were instantly crushed by battalions of well-equipped riot police.

The government was obviously anticipating trouble and taking precautions.

The reporters were having to fill the twenty minutes it took the justices to read out their judgements off-camera, and the arguments for and against were rehashed for viewers for the thousandth time. No one from Yokadus had agreed to speak to anyone in the media. Larry had issued strict instructions to that effect. He no longer wished to indulge in any intellectual justifications of his decisions. He simply intended to do what he believed was right for the company, without further discussion, confident that enough of the world's population would be on his side to make the product into the world-beater he now needed to justify the colossal investment he had been forced to make. He wanted the whole company to focus their efforts on preparing for the launch.

Without knowing what time the decision would be handed down, Julia and Carole had no option but to listen to all the arguments again, both the truths and the untruths, as they were picked apart by the professional pundits. If only it were as simple as the media made it sound. They both knew that the real problem was that there were few absolute truths or absolute untruths to be found anywhere. Mostly it was a contest between a variety of unknowns and speculations. What might happen in the future, whichever way the judgement went, was anyone's guess.

Julia, however, was very clear in her own mind that the gravest injustice would be perpetrated on the world's poor if things were to go in Larry's favour. Sitting with her mother in the quiet house, knowing that her father was dying in the next room, made it the most emotional day of her life. She was relieved she was there, out of sight, and not standing outside the supreme court in the glare of the television lights.

"We have just heard that Jim O'Neill may have an update," the reporter announced and Carole turned up the volume. "Jim, what have you got?"

"John, the court has ruled in favour of Geoff Madison and against Yokadus. We have no further details at this point. The people, it seems, have won. Larry McMahon is not going to be happy about this, John. Not happy at all."

Julia and Carole stared at the television, not daring to look at each other, the tears rolling down both their faces. Matt and Doug stood behind them, both equally lost in their own thoughts. They could hear the cheers rising from the crowd outside the court. People were embracing one another and jumping around with glee. The defeated looked more thoughtful than angry. In reality they had lost very little, but they had truly believed they had something to gain by the judgement going the other way.

Bit by bit, the judgement of the court emerged into the public arena, and the true concerns of the justices were broadcast to the world. Julia caught the odd phrase and the occasional word as they flew past: "the abuse of science"; "ungodly behaviour"; "immediate cessation"; "impounding"; "confiscation", "criminal prosecutions".

They were exactly the words she had prayed to hear. What she had feared most was a politically expedient or feeble judgement. She wanted the justices to spell out in very clear and unambiguous terms that this was one scientific advance that had gone too far. She and Carole embraced silently for what seemed like a long time as Matt and Doug stood back and waited respectfully, both unsure what to say to their mother and sister at such a moment.

"We should tell him," Julia said eventually.

"You tell him," Carole said. "It's your moment of victory as well as his."

Wiping away the tears, Julia made her way to the study, with Carole and her brothers close behind. They sat together by Geoff's bedside, listening to his laboured breathing. Julia lifted his limp hand.

"Can you hear me, Dad?"

To their surprise, he whispered back, "Did we win?"

"Yes, yes. We won, Dad. We won."

Carole cradled his head close to hers and she heard one last gasp from his chest, which sounded like, "An end to trading in time."

The heart monitor in the corner of the room went flat but nobody moved, not even the nurse. This was the moment Geoff had fought for – the absence of the right to live for ever.

In the other room, CNBC cameras had moved to the Yokadus headquarters as FBI agents and the military moved in to secure the building and seize their files as directed by the court. Larry and several of his senior executives were seen being led from the building in handcuffs.

Acknowledgements

I would like to thank Andrew Crofts for his excellent editorial advice and for cutting and polishing some rough diamonds.

About the Author

Owen Martin graduated in business from Trinity College, Dublin. He now lives in Switzerland and has spent most of his life in executive leadership positions worldwide. He travels extensively for business and writes occasionally for relaxation.

Find out more about RedDoor
Press and sign up to our
newsletter to hear about our
latest releases, author events,
exciting **competitions**
and more at

reddoorpress.co.uk

YOU CAN ALSO FOLLOW US:

 @RedDoorBooks

 Facebook.com/RedDoorPress

 @RedDoorBooks